A WAKE AND OTHER GHOST STORIES

GERARD LARKIN

TABLE OF CONTENTS

For my father whose old yarns haunt me still...

A WAKE

The chill from the open front door had crept into my bones; my fingers and feet were solid ice. Despite a dearth of visitors, you never closed the front door of a wake house. I lifted saucers and cups of half-drunk tea from side tables and from the mantlepiece. Clara would have had a fit if anyone had set a cup of tea on her polished mantlepiece. Any further visitors seemed unlikely at such a late hour; I pushed the door towards the frame, careful not to close it, after straightening up the black silk bow hung on the gleaming brass knocker. Checking the door was still slightly ajar, I returned to the parlour where my godmother lay in repose in her coffin in the bay window. I eased the parlour door shut. Before I sat down, Great Uncle Jack asked, "Is it a dry wake she wanted?"

"I don't know. I think I saw a couple of beers in the fridge," I said.

"Not at all, sure, beer repeats on me terribly. Have you not got a wee drop of whiskey just to warm us up?"

The room erupted in laughter. Typical of Great Uncle Jack.

After opening and closing various cupboards, I found a dusty bottle of *Jameson* whiskey on the sideboard. I poured a little of the bottle into a cut-glass tumbler and handed it to Jack. His eyes widened.

"You'd not insult me with that? Two fingers at least, son!"

I knitted my brows, not understanding his meaning, until he snatched the bottle, gripped the base of the glass and poured whiskey until it reached the top of his second finger.

"Two fingers," he said and took a long sip. He sat back in his chair, reaching behind himself to adjust the cushions.

"It always brings me back, you know? A wake," he said.

"What's that, Jack?" I asked.

1

"Willie's passing, God rest him."

"I'm sorry, Jack, it must be hard still?"

"He was a great fella, you know. I always thought that it should have been me."

"Ah, don't say that now," I scolded him.

He was still a while, gazing at the coffin.

"You'd think she was just asleep there," he said.

"She looks very peaceful, right enough," I replied.

"It was a strange thing at Willie's wake. Did I ever tell you?"

"No, Jack. What happened?"

"It was so long ago, but it's never left me," he began.

At twenty years of age, Willie had been six years older than Jack. Being the only sons of a family of nine children, they were as close as two brothers had ever been despite the age difference. Jack had just started working in the same factory as Willie and took his role as a working man of the family very seriously. At the end of his second week at work, Jack and Willie parted ways at the door to the bar in town where all the factory men spent their Friday evenings. Jack was disappointed to be left at the door, but Willie had promised to make up for it by taking him fishing the next morning. At daybreak on that cold Saturday morning in November, Jack hauled Willie from his bed. A weary-eyed Willie had protested, but they both knew he would never let his brother down. The young men took a bus with their fishing tackle as far as they could and walked the remaining five miles to the river. Jack could see his brother was exhausted, but a promise was a promise. They spent a fruitless hour fishing before Jack's line snagged. Thinking he had a bite, he hauled and heaved at the line.

"Careful!" shouted Willie just as Jack lost his balance and fell into the river. Immediately, Willie jumped in and pulled Jack upright before slipping on a rock himself and flopping hard to the riverbed. Thinking Willie was messing around, Jack laughed breathlessly until Willie did not stand back up. Jack dropped into the water and pulled at Willie. He grabbed him and dragged him to the riverbank, his shirt pink from the blood flowing from Willie's ear.

The wake was a sombre affair. Their parents were distraught having their strapping young son lying in a coffin in their parlour, as handsome as ever, a single bruise bloom on his temple, partially masked by the undertaker, the only sign that he wouldn't soon sit up, yawn, stretch and ask what was there to eat in the house.

John Mooney, Jack and Willie's first cousin, visited on the first night of the wake, both hands by his side, one grasping a white envelope. He walked to the coffin, blessed himself and said a silent prayer. He made the sign of the cross again, slipped a mass card from the white envelope, and placed it with the hundreds already surrounding the dead young man. When he turned to the family sitting in the parlour, tears streamed down his cheeks. He quickly rubbed his eyes with his fists. To Jack's father, he said, "Sorry for your troubles," and shook his hand. He embraced Jack's mother and repeated the words into her ear.

"Have a drop of tea," Jack's mother offered.

"Have you nothing stronger?" he asked.

"Jack, get John a bottle of *Red Heart* from the yard, son," said his father.

After a few deep slugs from the bottle of stout, John's rambunctious nature returned, and he regaled the mourners with tales of his and Willie's mischiefs as schoolboys in the same class. John's humour cut through the devastation in the wake house. As he handed Jack his second empty bottle, hand remaining outstretched for another, John looked at the clock on the mantlepiece with its hands stilled.

"Why is it stopped at quarter past twelve?" he asked, nodding at the clock.

An awkward silence filled the room before Jack's shaky voice replied, "That's the time he died."

John stared at Jack and back at the clock.

"But it couldn't be," he said.

"Why do you say that?" asked Jack's father, leaning in.

"Because I saw him at half twelve," John replied.

The mourners studied their hands, examined their feet, stared at the ceiling, looked anywhere but at John. He went on, "He called into the Railway. I was sitting at the bar and offered him a drink. He refused and said he wasn't staying. He told me to watch myself and said he'd see me soon. Then he left. I don't know why, but I remember looking at the clock behind the bar as he left – half past twelve. It stuck in my head for some reason."

"You've made a mistake, John," Jack's father insisted.

John knew not to argue with a man who had just lost his son and joked that maybe he shouldn't have been at the Railway door in the first place, waiting for it to open.

Willie was buried two days later. The funeral was huge, with so many young people, hearts breaking. Willie was well-known and well-liked. The whole family of hundreds of aunts, uncles, grandparents and cousins attended the mass, stood by the grave and met afterwards in the bar. One person was missing, however: John.

Once the sandwiches were eaten, the drink flowed, followed by the tears released as alcohol melted stoic facades. One of the neighbours had only started singing a sombre Irish song when she was hushed as the barman spoke to Jack's father. His pale-faced father announced that John's body was found at the side of a road; he had been knocked down and killed on his way to the funeral. Jack remembered then John's words, "He said he'd see me soon."

Great Uncle Jack wiped the side of his eye and held his glass up to me, "Two more fingers, if you don't mind?" My niece looked wide-eyed from Jack to me and from me to her mother. She slipped her arm into the crook of her mother's elbow. Breda, in turn, pulled her daughter close.

"Do you think those candles will last the night?" Breda asked, nodding at the two tall white candles burning in the neighbour's shiny silver candlestick holders sitting on a mahogany side table beside the coffin.

"There are more in the cupboard. I'll keep an eye on them. I'm sitting up tonight."

"Sitting up where?" asked my niece.

"You have to sit up with the deceased. They should never be left alone," I explained.

"Why?" she asked.

"Well, I don't know; it's just respectful, I suppose. It's the way things are done."

My niece looked unsure of my answer. I was pondering it myself when she asked another question.

"Why are the mirrors covered like that?"

I looked at the chimney breast with its old fireplace. The clock stopped on the mantle, and the mirror was shrouded in black silk.

"It's bad luck to leave a mirror, or picture, uncovered in a wake house."

"Why?" she asked, which seemed to be her favourite question right now.

"Some people say a bad spirit could appear in the mirror and take the deceased's soul to a bad place instead of heaven. Others say that if the deceased's soul sees him or herself in the mirror, it will be trapped in the house for eternity.

"They're just old customs, darling," Breda reassured her child.

"Brian, have you all the readings sorted for the funeral? Do you still want me to read a prayer of the faithful?"

"If you don't mind, Breda?"

"Of course, it's the least I can do for her. The last I can do for her..." her voice trailed off.

"Poor Clara with no children of her own to send her off," added Jack.

"She did alright," I said.

"True; she always loved you like her own," Breda said.

My throat tightened as childhood memories washed over me.

"I wish I'd been there more for her the last wee while, you know?"

Jack, Breda, my niece and I all heaved a collective sigh. The parlour was too quiet without the metronomic tick of the clock. Even the open window brought no din of traffic at this late hour. I was just about to tidy some things which I had already tidied three times when a noise halted me. I looked at the parlour door. We all glanced at each other. There it was again—footsteps in the hall. We were as frozen in time as the stopped clock. The old brass doorknob began to twist. At first, silently. Then, the creak of the spring. The door began to open into the room. We stared at the widening slit. Into the space glided a shape. All in black. I resisted the urge to leap away from the approaching figure. Into the room, it floated. Until the lamp light illuminated the wizened face of an old woman, she wore a black overcoat, her head covered with a tightly tied black headscarf.

"I've come to pay my respects," she said, her accent unplaceable.

"Of course, although it is late," I said, glancing uselessly at the stopped carriage clock.

She moved towards the coffin. I noticed that she had no mass card. My sister craned her neck to catch my eye behind the old woman's turned back.

"And how did you know Clara?" asked Breda.

"Ah, Breda, you've hardly changed at all since you were a wee girl. Are you still giving our Brian here a hard time so?" the woman asked, Breda's face reddening.

I asked the woman if she would like a cup of tea, but she seemed not to hear me.

"She looks so peaceful, just as if she's sleeping," she said.

"Will you take a sandwich, Mrs...?" Breda tried, hoping for a name.

"No, no, I'm not staying. Wouldn't want to waken old Jack there," she grinned, nodding at my Great Uncle, snoring in whiskey.

"Now, make sure you keep that window open," the old woman said as she glided out through the parlour door, closing it noiselessly behind her.

"Who was that?" my niece asked. I eased the door open and looked along the hallway to make sure she was gone, a shiver escaping from my spine.

"I have no idea, love," replied Breda.

"No idea!" I confirmed.

The strange old woman's visit seemed to steal any heat left in the parlour. I pulled on a jumper and fetched fresh candles. I lit the new candles from the flame of the guttering stumps in the silver holders. Molten wax spilt over my thumb as I changed them over.

"Jack, do you know her?" I asked my Great Uncle.

"Huh?" he replied, pulled back from another realm.

"Do you know that old woman who was just here?"

"What old woman?" he asked.

"Never mind," I said; he must have been asleep for her entire visit.

Breda unfolded a red tartan blanket and spread it gently over Jack's legs, but at her touch he leapt up so quickly he dropped his whiskey glass and kicked Breda on the shin. At her cry of pain, his wide eyes took in the room. He wiped the drool from his chin and said, "I'm sorry, love. I must have drifted off. It's my age, you see."

"It's alright," Breda winced, holding onto her leg and rubbing her sore shin.

My niece and I looked at each other. We had that knack of talking with our eyes. We had to look away, but our eyes flitted back. She broke first and ripped the tense atmosphere with her giggles. I followed. Breda was open-mouthed and angry, staring from one to the other, "It's not funny..." but she succumbed to laughter too. The laughter went on, ebbing and exploding until we were all tired and breathless.

"Sure, there you go, you need a good laugh at times like this," said Jack, "Your Granda was a wild man for the craic at wakes."

"Is that so?" I asked, never having met my Granda, who had died before I was born.

"When your Aunt Mini passed, God rest her, there was an uproar at her wake," he went on.

"Mini was a beauty in her day. She had long, silky black hair down to her waist and eyes as blue as the Atlantic on a summer's day. She had half the fellas in town wanting to court her and the other half pretending they didn't. Her feet were danced off her at the céilís and in the dances in the parochial hall. There were more than a few lads who came to blows over her. There wasn't as much drinking in those days, you know. You didn't need a drink anyway, there was that much craic at the dances. Out of all the young lads with an eye for Mini, the only one she had a soft spot for was Anthony Holland. The only problem was that Mini had taken the Pledge, she would not tolerate a drop of drink, but Anthony was awful fond of the beer. He eventually asked Minnie to walk out with him. She agreed, on the condition that he was to stop drinking. She was such a beauty that it would have been a small sacrifice for any man in his right mind. And all went well for a few weeks. They were seen regularly at the parochial hall and afterwards in Felloni's ice cream shop. They'd been getting on so well that Mini invited Anthony to meet her mother and father before he took her out on Saturday night. Now, your Granny was a formidable woman, and there weren't many, if any, who'd cross her. Anthony's nerves were wrecked, so he called into the bar for a quick one to settle his nerves. Well, he must have had some nerves because he could barely walk in a straight line by the time he called to pick up Mini, an hour late into the bargain. Mini's mother took one look at him, staggering up the path and sent Mini's father out to send him on his way. That was that and the end of the courting. Mini soon met Frank, and they had five children, but Anthony never married; he never got over Mini. She was well into her late 70s when she died, leaving behind her children and fourteen grandchildren.

The second night of the wake, once again up the path staggers Anthony, a few drinks in. By the time he reached the parlour, he was sobbing into his blue linen hanky. His heart was broken for his lost love, and there wasn't a dry eye in the room seeing how upset he was, even after all those years. He stepped up to the coffin, blessed himself and offered a prayer as he gazed at Mini's reposing face. Anthony was only a short fella, and the years had shrunken him even more. He stretched over to kiss Mini's forehead but couldn't reach. Determined, he pulled a stool over to stand on. Up he got, leaned over. The stool slipped out from under him, and he fell face-first into the coffin on top of poor Mini's body. The room was silent, everyone looking in horror at his kicking legs until your Granda, him nearly a hundred himself, says, "Poor Anthony, still head over heels for my daughter!"

Great Uncle Jack wheezed and wiped tears from his cheeks as Brenda and I erupted in laughter. My young niece stared from one to the other of us, incredulous, guilty.

"It's just a wee joke, love," Brenda said, "she wouldn't have wanted all tears and no laughter. It's the way wakes are here; you need laughter to balance the tears."

My niece considered a moment; she asked, "So you can laugh at a wake but not look in a mirror?"

"You can look all you want, as long as you're alright with the deceased soul being stuck in the house for all eternity!" said Jack.

"Really, Jack, that's enough," protested Breda.

"If the child is old enough to ask the question, she's old enough for the answer."

Breda rolled her eyes; "Come on, Jack," she sighed, "I'll give you a lift home. It's late."

Jack placed a hand on either arm of the chair and pushed and pulled himself to as upright a position as a man of his advanced age and porous skeleton could manage, never mind the whiskey sway. Breda and my niece hugged me before each taking an elbow of the old man who swatted them away as if they were two annoying buzzing bees. As he clasped my hand with both of his, he pulled me towards him and said into my ear, "Remember to keep the mirrors covered."

If the house had been quiet before they had left, it was now deathly silent and still. I cleared the remaining glasses, cups and plates into the kitchen; the rattle of crockery crashing through the quiet, the creak of the door deafening, and my shoes screeching on the polished parquet floor. I washed and dried the dishes as if trying not to disturb a slumbering child, the way that Clara would have tiptoed around me as a napping baby when she looked after me whilst my parents worked. After looking around the place to check that everything was in its place, as Clara would have demanded, I stood in front of the coffin. I wondered if I was supposed to talk to her. The visitors had been right; she did look like she was sleeping and yet not quite. She wasn't in the coffin; her body remained, but Clara was gone. Alone with that

10

realisation, I allowed my eyes to finally fill and spill over. I heard my cries as if they were coming from someone else, so unaccustomed was I to crying. People talk about a breaking heart, and I know no other way to describe the feeling of your heart cleaving in two in your chest. As suddenly as they came, my tears stopped, my blurry eyes cleared as the rivulets on my cheeks chilled in the cool breeze from the open window beside the coffin.

I took a cardigan from my overnight bag, pulled it on over my jumper, and sat beside the coffin. I wasn't sure what to do. I touched her hand, cold, smooth, like the fine bone China teacups she insisted upon. I began to pray the rosary, "Hail Mary, full of grace..." I counted the prayers on my knuckles, not having had the foresight to bring my rosary beads, a chain of beads in a tiny red leather pouch with Lourdes stencilled in gold on the flap, the pouch unopened since the day of my confirmation when Clara gave them to me with one hand, the other slipping a ten-pound note into my blazer pocket without my mother seeing. I smiled at the memory, trying to remember if I had just said my sixth or seventh Hail Mary. I would say an extra one, just in case.

When I had finished the rosary, I moved onto the leather wingback armchair. Her tartan blanket was still folded neatly over the back of the chair. I drew it around myself, inhaling the floral scent of her perfume. I felt as if I was once again the boy who ran into her arms at the school gate as she collected me at the end of the day, telling me that the baby was on its way. Later, my fingers were dripping with butter from the thick toast she made when she answered the beige Bakelite telephone to my father, calling from the hospital with the news of Breda's birth.

As the memories floated in and out of my mind, I felt my eyes draw together. I mustn't sleep. My duty to Aunt Clara was to sit up with her sleeping body, keeping watch. Awake. A wake. I lifted myself out of the armchair and stretched my arms over my head. "Arms up, stick them up," she used to say to me when helping me change my sweater. I smiled as I shook myself awake, the memory dragging my heart deep into my chest. Wiping away a single tear, I made my way upstairs into the little bathroom at the top. Clara's bedroom door was slightly ajar. Inviting me in. Something stopped me.

No, I mustn't go in. I remembered my wash bag was still downstairs. I went into the kitchen and lifted the tan leather wash bag from atop the fridge where I had set it earlier out of the way of tidying hands. I held the bag in my left hand as my right held onto the bannister, hauling my heavy body upstairs. I reached the top step. As I laid my hand on the bathroom doorknob, I glanced to my right. Clara's bedroom door was wide, a dark gloom hulking in the doorway. I moved my weight from one foot to the other. Wasn't that door almost closed not five minutes ago? Nerves shaped my hand into a tight fist. I strode across the landing to pull the door shut. When I reached the room, I saw the glint of her mirror. I walked in, lifted Clara's dressing gown from the back of the door and quickly draped it over the mirror. Closing the door behind me, the hairs scrabbled up my neck.

I closed the bathroom door tight and sat on the toilet, looking through my wash bag. I filled the sink and washed my face quickly, my eyes unwilling to stay shut too long. My hand reached for the pink towel which is always folded over the little towel rail beside the basin. I fumbled. The towel fell to the ground. I bent down, eyes picking out the towel on the black and white chequered tiles. I lifted it to my face and rubbed hard, standing upright. I opened my eyes and looked into the mirror. I stumbled back and fell into the bath with a screech. What I saw in that mirror would be branded on my mind forever. At first, I saw only my own familiar face. But then, just to the left was another face. This face was engulfed in flames. My face on fire.

Why the hell hadn't I thought to cover that mirror? Sure, it was only an old superstition, I thought. Until I saw my doppelganger with his face on fire. What could it mean? Still grasping the towel, I pulled myself out of the bathtub and threw the towel over the mirror without risking a second look into it. I hurried downstairs, grateful to notice Clara's bedroom door was still shut.

I burst into the parlour before remembering that this was awake and deserved reverence. I eased the door shut and quickly poured myself a large whiskey. The bottle almost fell as I fumbled to push the cork back in. I sat down with the glass held in both hands, trying to steady my breath as I sipped it. The more I replayed the image in my mind, the more ridiculous it seemed. It must have been a trick of light. Maybe I had some water in my eye. I convinced myself I had imagined it, imagined the image of my burning face. An image seared into my mind regardless. I have to admit that I refilled my tumbler more than once and eventually succumbed to a deep sleep until dawn split the drawn curtains above Clara's coffin.

I did not tell anyone about what I had seen, or imagined in the mirror, not even when Breda joked about the depleted whiskey bottle and about my fastidiousness at covering even the bathroom mirror. Clara's funeral was a quiet, beautiful and fitting send-off for a wonderful lady. Winter came, and Christmas arrived. It was a subdued affair, with Clara absent from Breda's Christmas dinner table. Although we raised a sherry to her after dinner, Clara's name was loudly unspoken throughout the festivities. When the bells on BBC One struck midnight on New Year's Eve, I choked back a sob, realising I was no longer needed to first-foot Clara's threshold with a little bag of salt and a piece of coal, as I had been doing since my father bequeathed me the duty when he had died ten years earlier.

The rest of the "firsts" came and went with varying degrees of difficulty. One year became two, and two were soon five years since Clara left us. Clara's anniversary fell halfway between Halloween and Christmas each year. A week after Clara's fifth anniversary, I had arranged to meet an old friend who had returned home from Australia for Christmas. Like so many young Irish people, Stephen had gone to Australia in search of work and a better life. He had left Belfast as an unskilled labourer almost twenty years ago but was returning with his own business. His wife and two children had stayed behind in Australia, wary of The Troubles. As I walked from the bus stop through the city centre, I saw the first Christmas trees and coloured fairy lights beginning to brighten up some of the dreary shopfronts and thought to myself how Christmas seemed to come earlier every year. The blurred reflection on the wet pavement of the fairy lights on the huge Christmas trees from the windows of The Continental Hotel twinkled, an irresistible jolt back into childhood.

Walking alongside the plate glass windows, I imagined I could feel the heat from the amber glow within, the glass steamed, blurring all inside. Front and centre of the hotel were massive revolving glass doors. I grasped a long, polished brass handle and stumbled as I lifted my head. Reflected back at me was my face. And another face. Engulfed in flames. My own burning face. I swooned. My arm was grabbed. I stared into the eyes of a top-hatted doorman dressed in deep green livery.

"Are you ok there, sir?" he asked.

"My face…" I replied, patting my jaw, cheeks, forehead.

"Your face?"

"It was on fire."

The doorman stared.

"I think you might have had enough for one night," he said.

"Enough? Drink, you mean? I haven't had a drink at all. I was just about to when…"

The doorman turned his head from me to the revolving door and back again.

"C'mere," he said.

I stood up unsteadily. Moved to the door.

"Look in the glass. See? It's your reflection, repeated in the doors."

He was right; there was my face, and behind it, my face again. Beyond were flickering electric wall lamps, flame-shaped bulbs within. The doorman laughed. I laughed too. Until I remembered. The wake. The same image in Clara's mirror. I stuttered thanks to the doorman, turned and hailed a taxi home. The driver eventually gave up his efforts at conversation after a clatter of one-word replies. My mind tried to compare the two scenes. What I saw reflected on the revolving glass doors of The Continental Hotel was exactly what I had seen in Clara's uncovered mirror during her wake. How could I be sure though? How could I compare two mental images? I was measuring memory against memory. Did what I saw in the glass doors remind me of my vision at Clara's wake? Or did Clara's anniversary suggest the memory of my burning face in her mirror and implant that over my face and some lamps? Obviously, Clara's anniversary, her more like a mother than an aunt, was an emotive time. My brain must be tired and susceptible to fantasy.

When I reached my front door, I was glad to live alone; to avoid having to explain myself, to be able to go straight to bed without question. In bed, I tried to read a few pages of a new novel by a Dublin author, which I had borrowed from the library, *The Commitments*. My bookmark was a memory card for Clara, a little laminated rectangle with her face and a prayer printed on it. Her face always settled me, and a contented sleepiness overcame me. Waves of gratitude for Clara softened my anxiety until I fell into a deep sleep.

I slept more soundly that night than I had for weeks. The next morning being, Saturday, I allowed myself a lie-in. At nine, I shaved. Downstairs, I filled a teapot, placed it on the hob, put two rounds of bread into the toaster, and went to the front door to pull the newspaper from the letter box. I set the folded paper on the kitchen table and brought my breakfast over. I sat down and slathered toast with butter, took a bite, gulped the hot tea and unfolded the newspaper.

CONTINENTAL HOTEL DESTROYED IN FIREBOMB! THREE DEAD. DOZENS INJURED.

I had to read it twice to be sure; The Continental Hotel, where I would have been last night, was firebombed. The telephone shrilled through my silent house. I knew before I answered it what the news would be. Breda stuttered it down the line. Stephen was dead.

If I had been with him, I would be dead too if I hadn't had that vision. If I hadn't looked in the mirror at Clara's wake…

WOOD

I know that many families, on Christmas Day, after the festivities of the big Christmas meal, like to gather in front of the television and watch the Queen's speech. Being in possession of passports of Heaney's green, we had little interest in the Queen's ruminations; instead, after dinner was eaten, dishes washed and dried, and the diminished Christmas table rearranged, we would don warm coats, hats, scarves, and walking shoes and stroll off our swollen bellies. I read recently, ironically, that this is the preferred post-dinner activity of the Queen too, on Christmas Day. Presumably, she finds her speech as hard to watch as many of us on the Other Island do.

Coming home from our walk, we would stoke the fire and pull together a supper of cold meats, stuffing, bread, and those little jars of unusual condiments which seem to appear exclusively at Christmas. Every year, the elder relatives, glass in hand, would take turns to share with us family tales of ghosts and things quite unexplainable.

Our house was an old three-storey red brick building. It was one of those with rooms off rooms that would never be built by the profit-minded builders of today. It was still single-glazed and draughty, even in summer. There was a limit to how long we could cheerfully call the Christmas dining room cosy and festive. Hot water rattled through cast iron radiators, depositing little in the way of heat on its journey. My father, always thrifty, would not allow the discreetly placed electric bar heaters to burn long after food was eaten. The drawing room, however, was magnificent. A Christmas tree as high as the ceiling stood in the bay window. A long Chesterfield sofa and various wingback armchairs provided seating for the adults, but my sister and I would pull huge, embroidered cushions onto either end of the hearth and have the best view of the storyteller and the hottest seats in the house beside the roaring fire. We would sit, enraptured.

And so it was that last year, after walking the little hill behind our house, we found ourselves in our traditional places, awaiting this Christmas's tale of terror from days gone by. Christina, my sister younger than me by one day less than a full year, was at that stage of adolescence when girls begin to dress like little women. I had the sense that she struggled to get as comfortable as she normally would on her cushion on the hearth, constricted, as women are, by feminine attire.

The weather that winter had been unpredictable: bitterly cold patches chasing days of unusually high temperatures. Despite a mild start in December, almost overnight, an icy dampness had settled on the house. In the drawing-room, a bottle of uncorked red wine stood in front of the leaping flames, its fruity aroma dancing with the scent of Christmas fir. The sky was pendulous with creamy clouds. Christina and I had kept a vigil on the bay window for even a flicker of a snowflake. By late afternoon, as darkness crept in, a bolt of lightning slapped the hill and the dogs howled as we held our breath, listening for the smack of thunder.

When the rain fell, the curtains were drawn, glasses topped up, chocolates and mince pies passed around, a tartan-checked woollen blanket draped over my elderly aunt's lap, and we waited for this year's storyteller.

"Did you know about the fairy tree in the garden?" asked Uncle Hugh.

"What's a fairy tree?" asked Christina, "We are a bit old for stories about fairies, Uncle Hugh!"

"These are Irish fairies, the Little People, and they're nothing like those sweet fairies you'd find in England, or God forbid, the leprechauns mincing about Disney films!" said Uncle Hugh.

"What is so special about Irish fairies," asked Christina, with a barely contained eye-roll.

"Agnes, have you taught these childer nothing? Irish fairies aren't really fairies, not in the way most people think of fairies. There is nothing cute about them; they are cunning, conniving and sometimes downright evil. Have you heard of the banshee? From the Irish "fairy woman." you'd not be wanting one of those at the bottom of the garden. The word "fairy" is one translation; "of the other world" might be a more accurate meaning. Rid yourself of any notion of Tinkerbell when you think of a fairy tree.

The Irish revered trees, believing some trees to be magical or even divine. I'm sure you've seen a single tree growing in an otherwise perfectly ploughed field. That is a fairy tree. Sometimes, they are surrounded by a ring of stones at the base. No one knows who puts the stones around the trees or why. You must never harm a fairy tree. Terrible bad fortune will befall anyone who attempts to cut or move a fairy tree.

Thomas O'Neill built this house. He was married to your great-great aunt Eunice. Theirs was a mixed marriage: him, a Presbyterian, and her, a Catholic. Although laws forbidding Catholics to marry Protestants had long since been repealed, it was still a very unusual thing in those days to marry outside one's faith. Most people disapproved. But a man more devoted to his wife no one had ever seen. After ten years of marriage, they were still not blessed with children. Although their love was devout and more than enough for Eunice, Thomas felt he was to blame and made it his life's work to compensate Eunice for his failings. They had a comfortable house in town, but Thomas took it into his head that Eunice deserved a special house built to impress their family and friends. Thomas bought this very plot of land just outside of the town and work began on plans and clearing the field. A great Christmas party was planned for their family, a tradition I suppose we continue today in our own way.

Eunice was busy planning the party and ordering drapery and furniture. She did not notice Thomas become a little withdrawn or that work on the house had stopped. The builders, you see, unknown to Eunice, had approached Thomas to tell him that they had discovered a tree ringed by stones on the plot, and they could not remove it. The tree was growing in the middle of where the house was to be built. Thomas did not believe in such superstitions, but his men did, and they were clearly agitated. He deliberated on moving the house to another part of the plot of land but finally decided that he could not compromise. He told the builders to remove the tree or find other work. They downed tools and left the site. Thomas himself chopped down the tree, dug out the stone circle, and hired workers from another town. His house was built exactly as he had planned. It was stunning and admired by all who happened upon it. He could not hear the local people's gullible whispering.

On the night of the Christmas party, Thomas announced to the guests that he was the happiest man alive. Men in those days were not given to public displays of sentimentality, but Thomas's eyes brimmed as he revealed that, until a few days ago, he cared nothing for possessions or any person other than Eunice, who was his whole life. Now, however, his heart swelled at the news that, after all these years, Eunice was expecting a baby.

No man had ever kept Christmas with such joy and contentment as Thomas did that year. Your grandmother always called the days between Christmas and the New Year the "dark days of Christmas" This proved prophetic. Just days after announcing the imminent birth of their long-awaited baby, Eunice, while surveying her winter garden, tripped and fell over an unseen stone. Her baby did not survive the fall. Whether due to the ensuing fever or grief, Eunice followed her baby to heaven before the sun rose on the New Year. Everything that Thomas had loved was taken from him within weeks of moving into the handsome house which stood atop the roots of the old fairy tree. The locals, unsurprisingly, knew exactly why tragedy had befallen Thomas."

We sat in silence after Uncle Hugh finished his tale until my mother scolded him for telling such a sad story, and on Christmas Day, too. Glasses were refilled, and soon Aunt Peggy was in full throat with *Down by the Sally Gardens.*

Uncle Hugh, with a remarkable sleight of hand, passed me a small whiskey, making a rare exception to his belief that water and whiskey were two divinely immiscible drinks. One should never pollute the other. The evening continued in a warm haze of candlelight, woodsmoke and song. Christina, I noticed, was quiet. I don't think she had spoken a word since Uncle Hugh's story.

Towards midnight, the room grew quiet, each of us at swim in our own thoughts as the fire splashed red and orange on our faces, dancing golden urchins reflected in our eyes. I watched my mother, her hands joined across her stomach as she contemplated Uncle Hugh. She must have wondered how many Christmases he had spent in this room, worried at the diminishing number of Christmases ahead of him.

A scream.

Mother leapt. Christina sat, gaping lips screeching. Her eyes were fixed on the old, gilded mirror which hung above the Chesterfield facing the fireplace. My mother pulled Christina to her chest, like a baby woken by night terrors, "What is it? Chrissie, what's wrong?"

"In the mirror," she trembled, "A branch!"

"What are you talking about? There's no branch in the mirror."

"There was!" she cried, "It grew out of the frame and reached for Aunt Peggy!"

"I didn't see anything, Chrissie," I said.

"Well, I did," she replied, turning her head towards our mother and sobbing.

When Christina's sobs had quietened and turned into the deep rhythm of sleep, we began to prepare for bed. Uncle Hugh switched on a lamp and blew out the candles. Aunt Peggy moved grimy glasses and plates into the kitchen whilst my father poked the fire, threw on shovels of slack, and placed the wire mesh fireguard on the hearth. One by one, as we made our way to the staircase, we bade each other a good night and a happy Christmas. Being unaccustomed to whiskey, polluted, or otherwise, sleep came quickly to me. It was, however, a fitful thing; almost hourly, I was awoken by what must have been a branch brought down in the storm. It scratched at the window with increasing ferocity until daylight chased it off.

St Stephen's morning began early and bright. A strong wind blew and chased any wisp of wind from the sky, leaving it an icy blue and slicing through every gap in the old house. It was tradition in our house for the women to lie on a little later on St Stephen's Day whilst the men made breakfast. After breakfast, some of us strolled to the quay in the village to watch the annual swim. My mother drove Aunt Peggy and Uncle Hugh in the car. Despite the whipping cold, the midwinter swim was always a joyful event. I thought that one year soon, I might take part too. Not yet, though, I said to myself as the swimmers emerged from the sea, smiling and blue, quivering like broken sails.

We arrived back at the house before the car. We lit the fire and warmed up soup made from leftover ham and garden peas. My father read a book on modern Irish history which I had bought him. Christina and I played chess at the window, peering out every so often, prompted by rumbling bellies, for any sign of the car. Around three, as the light seeped out of the sky, my mother opened the door, ushering through Uncle Hugh, who had his arm around a shaking Aunt Peggy. Peggy had a bloody gash on her left cheek. I shuddered as my mother explained how the wind had lifted a branch from the road and hurled it at her car, breaking the window beside Aunt Peggy and stabbing her face.

Although shocked, Aunt Peggy rallied once she had been cleaned up and had a bandage applied. With the blood cleaned, the wound was smaller and less shocking, more of a deep scratch, and Peggy was able to eat, although she refused any medicinal wine.

That evening was subdued. After supper, uncharacteristically, Uncle Hugh asked for the television to be switched on. My parents were more readers than television viewers, so they settled on watching a BBC adaptation of an M.R. James story, *A Warning to the Curious*. We lit the now misshapen candles and piled the fire high. The adults shared port and daubed tiny crackers with foul-smelling cheeses. The million little lights on the towering Christmas tree sparkled hazily in the shadows.

Our reverie was interrupted by three solid knocks on the front door. We looked at one another. Who could be calling so late, unannounced? Although Christmastime often brought unexpected visits from family or old friends home for the festivities. My father arose and made his way to the front door to let the visitor in, closing the drawing-room door tightly behind him against the cold. When he returned minutes later, my mother stood to greet the guest, but my father opened the drawing-room door with no long-lost relative; instead, in his hand, he held a long, thin tree branch.

"Who was it, Tom?" asked my mother.

"There was no one at the door, just this branch on the doorstep," my father replied.

"Local lads having the craic," said Uncle Hugh, "no harm done."

I glanced at Christina. She was paler than usual, I thought. Aunt Peggy, flustered, "I don't know... something does not feel right."

Uncle Hugh stood up and left the room, banging the door. His footsteps thumped along the hallway. Minutes later, he returned, in his hand, a hatchet.

Christina screamed, "No!"

He lifted the hatchet and brought it down on the branch. The branch was unmarked. He grabbed the branch, wedged it between the floor and the wall, and struck it repeatedly. With each strike, it simply bent a little and bounced back into shape. My father snatched the hatchet from Uncle Hugh and raised it high above his head. With his left hand, he held the branch in place, and with almighty effort, he launched the hatchet at the branch. When metal struck the wood, a wail filled the room as the hatchet was flung from my father's grip, and the branch reverberated into the air. Time slowed as the hatchet sliced through the room on a path towards Aunt Peggy. She screamed and threw her arms across her face. The weapon swiped past her, past the huge Christmas tree, and struck the long red curtains in the bay window. The crash of the smashing glass pane filled the room. A great wind sucked the curtain out through the broken window.

My father raced over to the window. He stopped dead. He turned and looked at us. His face was that of a terrified child. He lunged at the window, pulled the curtain back into the room, drew it closed, and gripped the curtain tightly with both hands. Wordlessly, my mother went to him. She reached for his hands. He made no resistance. She tore the curtains wide open. A gush blew out all the candles. At the window was a huge, gnarled, sinewy face. Sometimes, terror is silent, so it was that evening until Aunt Peggy and Christina began sobbing. The face at the window was rigid, contorted, fear itself. Uncle Hugh switched on the ceiling light. We could now see that the face was neither that of a human, animal, or any living being, almost. Uncle Hugh opened the rest of the curtains in the bay window to unveil a great tree with its strong limbs clinging to the entire casement. What we saw was no face, but an unnatural cluster of wooden knots pulled into the tight-wrung face of a man dying in agony.

We moved as one towards the drawing-room door. I could almost hear our racing hearts beat amongst the quick breaths and muffled sobs. At the front door, my father fumbled with the locks and bolts securely tightened against the night when he had last closed it. When we eventually made it outdoors, and around the drawing room bay window, the red curtains flapped listlessly through the gaping window frame, unincumbered by any tree.

That night, I helped my father nail a sheet of wood over the broken window. We kept the lights on in the drawing room as Uncle Hugh helped my mother sweep the broken glass off the floor. The fire was raked out, and the fireguard placed tightly around it. The room was locked, and we had tea in the kitchen beside the old Aga. No matter how much wood we piled on the stove, we could not shift the chill from our bones. My mother talked about tricks of light, the howling wind confusing our thoughts. No one argued with her. Soon, we all went to bed, with the exception of my father, who said he would be up soon.

I did not sleep much that night, was glad when the morning began to light the gaps around my bedroom window. I dressed and made no sound as I crept downstairs. From the staircase, I could still see my father in the kitchen, head resting on his arms on the table in front of him, the ceiling light still burning above him.

As quietly as I could, I opened the front door and walked around to the drawing-room window. Spikes of glass fringed the sheet of plywood covering the broken window. I stood for a while, looking around me. The nearest tree was at least thirty feet away. At my feet, a glister caught my eye—the hatchet. I bent down to pick it up but dropped it to the ground at once. My hands were sticky with blood. I burst back into the house and into the kitchen. My father's head rested on his arms on the table in front of him. Below the table lay his legs, severed at the waist, in a pool of dark red.

DEVIL'S ENTRY

His pulse thumped through his head. The noise of his breath rushed through his own ears. Why was he stupid enough to agree to this? If he dared to reach out his arms, he could almost touch both walls on either side of him as he crept down the endless alley. There was no light above, the dim glow of a cloudy night blocked by the tall back-to-back terraces. The undulations of the hill on which the houses were built meant that he could not see the end of the alley. As his eyes began to adjust a little to the darkness, his ears picked up no sound beyond the alley, only his galloping heart and bolting breath. His screaming vital organs would give him away.

Lifting one heavy foot, he felt a tremor in his leg. He thought he might vomit. Turning back would be quicker than descending the length of the alley but they would make his life hell, more than usual, if he chickened out now. Focus. He turned his head to the left and could make out the pattern of the brickwork, maybe some graffiti, although he could not read it. If he just focused on following the pattern of the brickwork to the end of the alley, he could do it. One foot in front of the other, brick by brick, how many bricks did he move past with each stride? If he could stop the shaking in his legs, maybe he could take bigger steps and get out of there faster. Five bricks. Try for six. Six, good, maybe seven? As he stretched his right leg forward, something swept between his legs. A grunt behind him glued him to the spot. Turn or keep on moving? He had to see. Slowly, he twisted his body to look behind him. Two green eyes glinted in the darkness—a dog. The dog sniffed and dawdled back out of the alley. He was tempted to follow suit, but they'd know.

Reassured that the beast had been nothing more than a stray dog, he moved down through the alley at a steadier pace. Now he used his hand to feel along the brickwork towards the exit of the alley. Brick by brick, guiding him out of the dark alley. Until his hand touched something that was not brick. Something warm. Something breathing. Pulling his hand back, he swallowed a scream. He had no idea which end of the alley would be the quickest escape. He stood there frozen. The sound of his own breathing was inaudible over the rasping all around him, something between braying and growling. Then a rhythmic scraping, some tool against stone? A saw? Hooves pawing the ground? This beast, definitely not a dog, began to move around him, circling and circling. Slowly the beast stopped in front of him and raised two glowing red eyes. They seemed to stare deep inside him. The boy ran. Seeing a light ahead, he aimed for the far end of the alley. The creature followed. The boy outran the thing, although it could catch him if it wanted; it was playing with him. As he neared his escape, his eye was caught by a figure in a doorway, "Stupid boy," he hissed as he closed the door with a creak. Bursting out of the alley, under the safety of the orange streetlights, a crowd of boys slapped him on the back, jumped on him, shouting, "You did it! You legend! You did Devil's Entry!"

In the Belfast Blitz, part of a local primary school was bombed. Unfortunately, that part of the school building was being used as a makeshift bomb shelter at the time. Miraculously, only two people lost their lives. A third person, however, disappeared. A mother raised her head after the blast to discover her young son was no longer under her arm and nowhere to be seen. Local people searched the area to no avail. Most people accepted the theory that the boy had been hit by debris and, concussed, wandered off, never to be heard from again. His mother, a pragmatic woman, believed differently. Only days before the bombs began, her son had told the woman that he had seen strange eyes following him on his way home from school. In place of her missing son on the night of the bombing, lay a pristine playing card. The ace of spades. She believed he had been taken by someone who had stalked her son and dropped the playing card in their haste. When she shared this information with the parish priest, he offered mass for the boy's soul and told the mother that her son would not return. The woman keened that a devil had taken her son. The priest privately agreed with her words.

The boy's was the first disappearance to occur. When the school was rebuilt, its wall formed part of the boundary of the alley, which was to become known as Devil's Entry. Locals differed on whether the name originated from the mother's words or whether it was more literal. As the years went on, Devil's Entry was mentioned in the narratives of almost every child's disappearance, of which there were a significant number. Unsure if the malevolence was human or otherwise, parents warned their children to stay away from the Devil's Entry after dark, lest the Devil himself snare them.

Superstitions are universally irresistible to children, so many other theories and tales of Devil's Entry grew, along with the children, leaving few certain of what was fact and myth. Naturally, the group of boys who found themselves discussing Devil's Entry on Halloween night was probably not the only such troupe to do so at that very same time.

"My da said that his brother Ted saw the devil himself there and disappeared two days later," said Peter.

"You da says more than his prayers," said Tommy.

"Are you saying my Uncle Ted didn't disappear?" said Peter.

"No, I'm saying your da is full of…"

"Cut it out, Tommy!" shouted Gabriel, "Go back to your story, Pete."

"Loads of people have walked down Devil's Entry, but they don't all disappear, obviously. You have to actually see the devil, but even then, it's only if he marks your card," said Peter.

"Marks your card?" asked Gabriel.

Peter continued, "He leaves a sign. When he took the first boy, there was an ace of spades left behind. His ma thought that the devil had left it, but some people said that the wee lad had the card before the devil took him. One of his friends said that they had been playing a card game. Like Old Maid, you know where three of the queens are taken out and whoever is left with the remaining queen is Old Maid. Except the boys had been playing it using the aces and the ace of spades for the Old Maid card. Whoever ended up with the ace of spades had to do a dare. The wee fella got the ace, and they dared him to walk down that alley alone in the dark just a few days before the bombing."

"I heard it was the devil's hoof," said Tommy.

"What?" asked Gabriel.

"If you walk down Devil's Entry and he sees you, he comes to your house and leaves the print of his hoof to let you know you've been marked," said Tommy.

"Jesus, lads, I'll never sleep tonight!" said Gabriel.

"Are you up for it?" asked Peter.

"For what?" asked Gabriel.

"A game of ace of spades, and whoever loses has to walk the Devil's Entry. Tonight," said Tommy.

"No chance!" said Gabriel.

"Chicken!" shouted Tommy.

The boys went on goading, sneering, daring, and mocking until they all agreed to the game. No backing out. The game went quickly, and when Peter ended up holding the ace of spades, the colour drained from his face. Gabriel said they should make it the best of three. Unluckily for him, Gabriel held the following two aces of spades. He would have to walk Devil's Entry alone, in the dark, on Halloween night.

Gabriel stood at the upper entrance to Devil's Entry. "Look, this was a stupid idea. You don't have to do it," said Peter.

"Wise up, it's only a bit of craic. Away you go, Gabe," said Tommy.

Gabriel looked from one to the other and walked straight into the alley. They are all just silly kids' stories, he thought to himself. Not more than a few feet into the brick corridor, all light seemed extinguished. Behind him grumbled a cold wind. Above him, an owl hooted. The caw-caw of an unseen bird startled him. A crow in the dark? The caw-caw intensified as he moved further through the darkness, becoming deafening. A brush across his cheek. A wing? He ran forward. As the owl hooted, the bird cawed, and the wind roared, Gabriel was there but not there. His walk automatic, his thoughts drowned out by the hellish noise. Slowly, a snarl joined in the infernal cacophony.

In front of his eyes rose an unseen whirlwind, motes of dust scraping his face. The squealing of the unseen creatures pierced his ears. He covered his face with one arm and pushed through the alley, blinded and deafened. Gabriel was not brave, but he faced the terror head on. He pushed ahead until he was knocked off his feet. He tried to stand. Fell back down. His head had hit something hard, immovable. Touching his head, he felt the warm trickle of blood run down his forehead and along his eyebrow. Slowly, he reached out his other hand. He recoiled at the cold, hard object. His heart punched in his chest. He scrambled onto all fours and crawled towards the object. With both hands, he touched it. Felt the cold hardness of brick. He must have walked into a wall. Laughter exploded from his belly. The demonic orchestra had ceased. Gabriel lifted himself up and strode down Devil's Entry. As the streetlights grew brighter, just a few feet from the end, a hand grabbed his arm. "Stay out of here, stupid boys!" said the gravelly voice, before coughing violently. Gabriel did not stay to argue.

Peter and Tommy were waiting for him as he left the alley. "You were fast," said Tommy.

"Didn't feel like it!" laughed Gabriel.

"What did you see?" asked Peter.

"Nothing, it's all bull…" but before Gabriel could finish his sentence, the boys were rocked by a roaring wind tearing down the alley.

"I'm getting out of here!" said Peter, and he and his two friends sprinted home.

The next morning, the third day of the boys' midterm break, Gabriel woke late. He opened his bedroom curtains a little and saw a clear blue sky. The trees in the garden were clinging to their last golden leaves. Pumpkins outside of neighbours' houses shrivelled slightly, making their carved visages more gruesome. He lifted his mobile phone and saw he had three unread text messages from Tommy;

Are you awake, mate?

Gabe, are you there?

Are you ok, mate? Text me as soon as you get this please!

Gabriel's thumbs flicked out a reply. *Just awake, what's up?*

Instantly, Gabriel read that Tommy was typing;

Pete has disappeared.

What do you mean?

Called to his house, and his ma said he didn't come home last night.

WTF???

I need to talk to you, replied Tommy.

Come on over.

Gabriel got dressed quickly and scoffed a bowl of cereal with too much milk in it. When Tommy arrived, the two went to Gabriel's bedroom.

"What's going on?" asked Gabriel.

"Look, a couple of days ago, Pete was a bit freaked out. He said he'd seen something in Devil's Entry."

"When was he in Devil's Entry?" asked Gabriel.

"Like I said, a couple of days ago. He'd been hanging about with his older cousins, and they dared him to do it," said Tommy.

"Why did he not say anything last night?" asked Gabriel.

"He was freaked out. He said he saw something in that alley, but mate, I didn't believe him."

"Why did you two make me go down Devil's Entry? Seriously, where is he? There was nothing in that alley. Whatever he saw was his in his head," said Gabriel.

"That's what I thought, mate. I told him the same thing. I told him we'd get you to do it, too, and he would see it was all bull. But now he has disappeared."

"You're winding me up!" said Gabriel.

"I wish, mate. His ma is phoning the police," said Tommy, "and there's something else."

"What?"

"The devil's hoofprint."

"What?"

"Remember the part of the story about the victims' card being marked? Sometimes by a hoofprint? Well, when I was at Pete's house this morning, there was a hoofprint on his front doorstep."

"Shit!"

"What are we going to do, Gabe?" asked Tommy.

"We need to find Pete. This can't be real. He's scared himself. Maybe he's hiding somewhere. I hope he hasn't done anything stupid."

The boys spent the day in vain searching all their hangouts for Peter. He did not reply to any of their many texts, nor had he read them. In late afternoon, as late autumn darkness crept in, the boys parted, Gabriel reassuring Tommy that Peter would definitely turn up.

Gabriel returned home and went straight to his bedroom. He lay on the bed for a long time, searching his brain for a clue to where Peter had gone. As the light grew dimmer and Gabriel grew weary, he decided to nap. He turned on his side and pulled the pillow under his head. As he pulled his legs up to his chest, he noticed a glint where the pillow had been. He touched the thing and brought it to his eyes. A playing card, the ace of spades.

THE HEDGE SCHOOL

This road had been a deciding factor in accepting the job he was on his way to begin. The cobalt sea to the right and the sky above leaked into one another, vastness against which the dark, dusty rocks to the left jutted. The road writhed around the coast, a single lane in each direction, sometimes narrowing, barely a lane at all. The sea was held from the road, at times with thick tubular metal fences; at others, kept back with huge boulders which crumbled into stones and coarse sand, covered and uncovered by the undulating tide. At points, he drove past overgrown briars laden with salty blackberries. This road was his parents' summer Sunday driving route throughout his childhood. As a boy, he wondered if the beauty of the journey became dulled to the few residents dotted along the coast. As a man closing in on forty years of age, still enchanted by it, he could not imagine that one could ever fail to be moved by this rugged seafront.

The summer had mostly been a damp affair, but for these last few days of August, the sun was splitting the stones, as his mother would have said. Little coloured triangles floated on the distant sea, moneyed men from the city sailing their Sunday away. He pushed down the thoughts grabbing at him that he was making a mistake. He had not been in a classroom in six months, not since that poor girl. He focused on the road and looked for the rippling blur that rose from the tarmac on hot days; his older brothers had called the phenomenon an oasis, but he wasn't sure that was quite right. Rounding a corner, he saw the old white lighthouse teetering on the high cliff, the huge bulb a bird's eye stalking the little cars below.

Carved out of the cliff was a road which ran parallel to the main seafront road, before winding up the cliff. Abel turned left almost imperceptibly and swept into the trees which hid the road from the sea. The trees to the right bent over and touched the cliffs, creating the dark green tunnel through which he now drove, leaving the shimmering sea behind him. Although inland, the green tips of the horse chestnut trees had already started to fade, the heat was unnatural for this time of year, and Abel was glad to be shaded from the direct sunlight of the coast road. Between the trees, a little cross reached into view, followed by the aged-green copper of a small spire. Soon, the grey-bricked church building emerged like a miniature Gothic castle. He glanced at the handwritten directions lying on the passenger seat. He was to drive through the gates and past the church and he would find the priest's house two hundred yards down a lane.

The afternoon sun reflected sparks of colour off the stained-glass windows of the cruciform church. He doubted the building could hold more than one hundred worshippers; the parish must be very small. The house, however, looked big enough to house ten priests. It was a white-rendered, double-fronted Victorian house with matching bay windows on each side of the wide black double doors, which were approached by three broad stone steps. A small lawn bordered the neat rose gardens which marked the boundary of the property, the manicured grounds abutting the wilderness of the coastal countryside surrounding the priest's house.

Abel parked his car in one of the two spaces to the right of the front doors and stepped onto the gravel drive. He strode up the steps and rapped the door firmly with the smooth, shiny knocker, much more confidently than he felt. He waited a few minutes and raised his hand to knock again when the door opened sharply.

"Yes?" asked a woman in a long dark skirt, beige, high–buttoned blouse and dark green apron, presumably the housekeeper.

"I'm Abel Keane, the new teacher..."

"Of course you are," she said and closed the door.

Abel stood on the step and looked around him. Had there been a mistake?

He stepped back and was about to leave when the door opened again, and a beige arm thrust a set of keys into his hand, "Back the way you came, a hundred yards on the other side of the church, you'll see the sign for St Joseph's Primary School."

She shut the door before he could thank her. What an odd woman, he thought. He would have appreciated a glass of water after a long journey on a hot day, but he dared not disturb her again and climbed back into his car and drove down the lane. Sure enough, before long, he spotted the blue school sign that he had missed on his way to the priest's house. Below the sign the padlocked school gate. Fumbling with the bunch of keys, after trying every key surely at least twice, he eventually found the one which fitted. The lock was rusty and stiff. The padlock had clearly been unbothered through eight weeks of the rain and sun of a wild Irish summer. The gate creaked open, and he walked down a short lane overhung with brambles clutching globs of red and purple fruit. As the path ended, St Joseph's came into view. It was a single-storey red brick building. In the centre was an arched porch closed off by a wooden double door, semi-circular at the top. On either side were two tall, narrow windows. At each gable end of the building were two wooden canopy roofs with writing etched in the stone lintel beams, "Boys' Entrance" and "Girls' Entrance."

As Abel went to the locked teacher's door, he could not resist feeling the old red brick, the heat absorbed from the sun and the rough texture on his smooth fingertips. It was a beautiful building; he felt like he had known it all his life, standing here as if he had stood here day upon day for years. Yes, he thought, this was the right decision. The lock in the wooden door opened easily. The old brass was well polished, and his hands shone a brassy gold in the reflection. He pressed the heel of his hand against the grainy wood and readied himself to put his weight behind the door to open it, but to his surprise, the doors opened wide of their own accord. He must have pushed. The heat of the old red bricks had not made its way indoors; his breath misted in the room before him. The space directly in front of him would have been the main school room, and to his left, a tall, floor-to-ceiling wooden wall was held in place by metal tracks in the ceiling and floor. He has seen similar contraptions in university; moving walls to separate a room into two smaller rooms. At one end of the moveable wall was an ill-fitting door joining the two spaces. He inhaled dust and tasted the mustiness of it on his tongue. Every floorboard groaned under his footsteps as he crossed to the opposite side of the room. The foliage on the other side of the windowpanes was gauzed by grime, making the views not quite real, as if seen on screen. Inside the schoolhouse, he was set apart from the hot, buzzing thrum of the countryside he had just driven through. Still, the cold was a pleasant respite from the Indian summer.

Abel set about cleaning the room. He hadn't seen a blackboard since the early days of his teacher training, but this room had only a massive black chalkboard, no sign of a modern drywipe whiteboard, and certainly no interactive whiteboard. Even two months after chalk had last marked the blackboard, its dust still hung in the air, sunshine breaking through the filmy windows and creating beams of chalky specks. The suspended fragments hung in the space like time frozen in this room. He could hear his own breath. Every item he touched made an echo around the building. From under the teacher's desk, he couldn't remember the old master's name. He lifted a dustbin and walked around the room. Despite the neat, orderly first impressions, the room harboured a host of secreted clues as to its inhabitants. On one windowsill sprawled a half-dried-up spider plant. When he lifted it to bring it to the sink to try and revive it, he noticed little scrolls of wood curled like concertinas, shavings of coloured pencils hidden amongst its leaves. Behind the water tap at the sink was a single lid of a felt-tip marker. He lifted it and looked around for a pot holding its owner. He spotted a tall bookcase with teachers' manuals on the top shelves – curriculum documents, books on classroom management, lever arch files, a Latin reader and a book of poetry in Irish. At pupils' waist height, a shelf was laden with cylindrical pots of different colours with pencils, markers, scissors, crayons, glue sticks and fountain pens. There were no exercise books of children's work to help him gauge where to start work with them, but he supposed some teachers sent those home with the pupils at the end of term. It occurred to him that there were none of the usual technological devices to be seen, which education college lecturers and school inspectors made such a fuss of being part of every lesson, no electronic tablets, no PC, no laptops, not even a box of calculators. At this point, Abel half-seriously began to wonder if the pupils he would soon meet had still been using chalk and blackboard, too. He smiled, imagining barefooted children in Victorian dress practising their cursive letters on little individual blackboards with sticks of chalk. He thought then how nice it would be to teach lessons without having to shoehorn an activity on an iPad into a lesson on reading. Back to basics had a lot of appeal after the year he had had.

Abel spent two hours planning lessons for the first day. He had found some paper and planned to have the students write about themselves to assess their writing and get to know them better. He found some comprehension books from the 1980s and grouped them into neat piles according to difficulty. Realising that he had not yet found a photocopier or a computer, he decided to write some mathematical problems and sums on the blackboard but could not find any chalk. He opened the desk drawers and found them mostly empty, save for a few paper clips and lidless ballpoint pens. On the shelves, too, there was no sign of chalk. On the ledge of the blackboard was an old wooden duster but no chalk. He had just decided to give up for the day, lock up, and implausibly find a shop that sold chalk when the front door swung open.

"Hello, hello! Mr Keane? It's Father McBride. You can call me Malachy now, if you like, or Father Mal, or whatever you like!" laughed the figure in black silhouetted in the doorway.

Abel shaded his eyes as he looked up at him, "Yes, I'm Abel."

"I should hope you are," laughed the priest. It was not the first time a stranger had found mirth in his homophonic name. Abel smiled, "Pleased to meet you again, Father." In his experience, priests enjoyed the deference.

"My apologies for not bringing you down here myself. I was in the garden, you see. Lynn should have let me know you'd called."

"Not at all, Father McBride. It was great to have a bit of time to do some preparation for Monday."

"Great diligence. I love to see it," said the priest. "It's only a wee school, but we are very proud of it in the parish. The Department tried to close it down, but we took it over, and it's entirely funded by donations to the parish finances, including your wages and those of Miss Mooney, your assistant. She's paid for four hours every morning, but she's always been very good and stayed on a bit when needed. As you can see, there is the capacity for two rooms, but seeing you'll only have twenty pupils, there'll be no need to use the second room. It would only be a waste of electricity and heating costs."

"Of course, you're right; one room is fine," replied Abel.

"Just as we're talking about minding the finances," continued the priest, looking into the corner of the room, "I don't think there's any need to waste the coal on such a warm day."

Abel followed the priest's eye and saw there, for the first time, a stove with a bellyful of smouldering embers.

Confused, Abel started, "But I didn't light that, why would I?"

Father McBride furrowed his eyebrows, "But who else would light it? There's no one else here."

Abel's words stuck in his throat, "Maybe Miss Mooney? Or your housekeeper?"

The priest laughed, "Miss Mooney is in Belfast till this evening, and Lynn has plenty to do in the parochial house."

"I've been so busy, I must have done it without even thinking," replied Abel, that familiar tight feeling in his chest.

The priest's eye contact was a little too steady, too deep, too knowing; Abel shifted his gaze to the blackboard, away from the priest and the stove. Father McBride walked towards the door.

"Don't stay too much longer here, Abel. You don't want to be exhausted before the school year even starts. And please, call me Malachy."

"Thanks, Father. Malachy."

The priest chatted with Abel as he locked up the school and gave him directions to the cottage he was renting. Abel couldn't remember much of what he was saying; his mind stuck on the fact that he hadn't even known there was a stove in the schoolhouse, so how would he have absentmindedly lit it?

The cottage was ancient, with stone walls and a roof which would originally have been thatched. He thought how pleasant it would be on dark autumn nights to be in this tiny home, fire lit, wind howling, and the sound of nearby crashing waves. As he unpacked his things and the night drew in, he realised that the cottage would likely be cold all year round and lit himself a fire.

41

He stared into the flames as he considered the schoolhouse stove. However, he had much to plan for his new class and put the thoughts out of his head that he was once again falling down that tunnel. Instead, he filled his head with activities for his new pupils.

The next morning was Sunday and as bright a day as the one left behind. Abel dressed in a short-sleeved, button-down shirt and formal trousers, ready for chapel on a hot day, knowing his attendance at mass would be observed every Sunday and any absence noted. He loaded a box of books into the boot of his car to drop off at the schoolhouse. When he arrived at the school, the lock on the gate opened more easily than it had yesterday but he made a mental note to buy some oil for it to get ready for autumn in any case. The short lane to the schoolhouse felt like a little glen, the tall green briary hedges sloping on either side of it, forming a little valley-like space. He looked to the tops of the hedges, trying to spot which birds were chanting such beautiful morning songs. So early in the day, the schoolhouse was bathed in sunlight. The two windows shone like eyes watching him approach. He carried the box to the doorway, set it at his feet and slipped the key into the schoolhouse door lock. The door swung open in silence. Abel lifted the box and walked towards the desk, his desk now he supposed. He stopped. Turned slowly. Was that a hand on his shoulder he had felt? The room was empty. Silly thoughts. He turned again and moved instead in the direction of the shelves to organise his books. Could he smell burning? He swivelled to examine the old stove, nothing but ash today. Another job to add to the list; clean and set the fire. Yet the smell lingered. The room just needed airing after yesterday's fire. Who had lit the fire was still on his mind. When he had finished organising the books, first by subject, then by size, he began to lift wooden chairs down from the school desks. Who would sit where? He realised that he did not have a class list. He had no idea which student was which age. He supposed he could take a list in the morning when they arrived. Maybe his assistant would know; didn't the priest call her Miss Mooney? He wondered what age she was. He felt more like a child before their first day at school than the teacher in charge. He had no idea what was in front of him. Doubt started to creep into his thoughts; was he doing the right thing? Was he ready to teach again? No, put those thoughts away. Being prepared was the best antidote to such anxiety. Abel walked to the desk and looked at his handwritten plan. Maths problems, chalk, he'd forgotten to buy chalk! As he silently cursed his forgetfulness, a curt click broke the silence. He looked up and saw on the floor a stick of chalk, broken in two. Above the fragments, on the blackboard ledge, two intact sticks of white chalk were lined up beside the wooden blackboard duster. His breath stuck. Abel was absolutely certain there had been no chalk yesterday. He had searched the desk, checked the blackboard ledge, and gone through the whole room. There was no chalk. Where had it come from? Cold fingers on his neck. He swiped at them. Turned. No one was there. He was rooted to the spot. Breathless. Sweat sticking his collar to his skin. Abel lifted the empty box and his keys and crossed the floor in two long strides. He slammed the door, locked it and jumped into his car. His heart pounded as he accelerated down the narrow country lane to the church.

He was too early for mass. He parked and entered the cool chapel, intending to light a candle. Inside, the walls were a pale pink. Paintings hung on the walls depicting the Passion of Christ. The altar was all marble and shiny brass, in contrast to the plain wooden pews for the congregation. To the top left of the church was a small recess in which were a few more wooden seats and a statue of the Virgin Mary, a votive stand at her feet holding rows of blue glass candle holders. On the opposite side of the church was an identical recess but with a statue of Saint Joseph carrying an infant Jesus and a votive stand of red glass candle holders. In the pew in front of the statue of Mary, an old lady wearing a headscarf knelt, working rosary beads through her arthritic fingers; he decided to go to the other shrine. He found change in his pocket, dropped coins into a wooden box beside the candles, lit a votive with a modern long-necked lighter and dropped to his knees in the first pew. With closed eyes, he started a few prayers but lost his way after a line or two. What was happening to him? Was it the schoolhouse? The lit stove made no sense. The chalk made no sense. Shortly, the chapel began to fill, and he took a different seat at the back of the church. People could be very possessive of their church seats, but he figured anyone who sat at the back would be less likely to be offended by the stranger in their pew.

During the service, he came to the conclusion that someone must be going to the schoolhouse without his knowledge. The mass was just thirty-five minutes long, for which he was grateful; he was less grateful when Fr McBride announced just before dismissing the congregation that the new schoolteacher, Mr Keane, was in attendance at the back of the church. His hopes for a discreet first church visit were dashed. After mass, the churchgoers gathered in chatting groups. Some eyed him, others introduced themselves. He was awful at remembering names and was overwhelmed by the friendliness, inquisitiveness and handshaking. He knew he was going to offend some of them when they came to drop off their children, and he could not remember their names. He made his way to the priest.

"Father, has Miss Mooney been at the schoolhouse?" he asked.

The priest barely looked at him as he was shaking hands with parishioners, "Miss Mooney? No, no, she missed the last bus from Belfast and won't be up until this afternoon. Don't worry. She'll be bright and early tomorrow."

"Um, ok, Father," said Abel, "thank you." He went to his car. If not Miss Mooney, then who? Abel arrived back at the cottage and ate a sandwich. Maybe he was paranoid, but looking back on this morning after mass, he thought some of the parishioners had a look in their eyes. Suspicion? Possibly, but more like a knowing. At the interview for the job, he had to explain why he had not taught in the previous six months. He assumed the information would be confidential, but had one of the interviewers broken confidentiality? Was the whole village talking about him? Was someone testing him by playing tricks on him at the schoolhouse? He could not remember who was on the interview panel other than Father McBride. His head swam with possibilities, so he decided to walk it off and get his bearings around the little town. It was another gorgeous day, with blue skies, and wisps of silky clouds floating above. It wasn't much of a village, no real main street, houses were old cottages scattered about the landscape, and roads led into lanes, many of which stopped dead at little cottages. If not for the telegraph poles and cars parked outside the bungalows, you could imagine you were transported to a hundred years ago. As he turned a corner, in the midst of the beauty sprawled a modern filling station, complete with a glass-fronted grocery shop. He strode into the shop and walked up and down the aisles. At the end of one aisle, he found a stand with everything from safety pins to hair clips. He looked up and down the stand and located boxes of chalk. He bought two each of white and coloured chalk. Finally, he thought, he was ready for his first day at school.

Monday morning, the weather had begun to break with fog around the village. Abel arose early, washed, dressed and ate a quick breakfast. He wanted to be at school long before the pupils. Given the fog, he abandoned yesterday's plan to walk to school and drove the short journey to the schoolhouse. As he pulled on the handbrake at the school gates, he saw a young woman in her mid-thirties standing at the gate: dark-haired, long skirt, blouse and oversized cardigan. She carried a large green leather bag on her shoulder. She smiled as he opened the car door.

"Good morning, Mr Keane. I'm Miss Mooney, Róisín, when the children aren't around," she said, stretching out her hand.

"Lovely to meet you. I'm Abel, but not in front of the children," he laughed, shaking her hand. She smiled widely.

"Are you not foundered in this fog? Have you no keys of your own to get inside?" he asked.

"There's only the one set of keys, Abel. Some of them are too old to have copies cut. And sure, I've this great cardigan!"

"Ah, right, of course," he replied, trying to hide his disappointment.

Miss Mooney proved to be a saviour. She knew all the children, and they clearly adored her. She discreetly helped Abel to remember their names and those of their parents who appeared more excited than their offspring to talk to the new teacher. The morning's lesson went well; he had never come across such well-behaved pupils. They ranged in age from seven to eleven years old, which was not as challenging as Abel had imagined, thanks to Miss Mooney's expertise, she even stayed on after their lunch break to help him for the first week. Abel thoroughly enjoyed his first day and found Miss Mooney to be easy, chatty company. She told him some of the history of the schoolhouse. It was known as locally as The Hedge School because it was built in the same place where covert school masters held classes behind hedges in the times of the Penal Laws when Catholic children were forbidden from going to school. When she left the schoolhouse, telling him not to stay too late, he enjoyed the silence and spent a few contented hours marking and preparing for the next day.

That September was as enjoyable a first month of school as Abel had spent since his first years of teaching. The pupils were well-mannered and appeared to enjoy every lesson he prepared. Already, he could see the younger pupils improve their word reading and spelling, the older children were hungry for complex Maths problems, and all the children were engrossed in the history lesson he was delivering with the help of the local librarian who directed him to all manner of books, pamphlets and booklets describing the history of the village for the last one hundred and fifty years. Country people seemed particularly protective of their local histories; many of them could trace their family trees back through time, weaving a rope that tied them to their history. Although the inquisitiveness could be grating, there was a sense of family in the little village, not only because so many of the locals were, in fact, related, which was evidenced in the lack of variety in their surnames, but the villagers looked out for one another, no door was shut to a neighbour, and no one was afraid to tell off a rowdy teenager or an unruly youngster. Abel felt safe, at least in the beginning.

October blew in off the sea. Sand gathered in drifts along the road edges. Further inland, the sea became visible as leaves shivered off the trees. As the days shortened, Abel felt his energy wane. He could not think of another way to help wee Eily Magee learn her five times tables. Sean Fox had finished his reading book but still struggled to read half of the words. He wasn't ready for the next book in the series, and the school didn't have any other reading schemes. Johnny Joe O'Donnell's mother cheerfully left him into school late every Friday morning at 9.30am, missing the spelling test, meaning Abel had to find time somewhere else to test him individually. Abel knew that some of the parents had it tough enough, working two jobs and still barely getting by, but Johnny Joe's mother never missed the Thursday night music session in the local bar, and he couldn't help thinking that might have some bearing on Johnny Joe's Friday tardiness. He was tired of writing exercises into the pupils' books because he had no photocopier or computer to produce worksheets. He had used the machines in Fr McBride's office a few times in September, but Lynn, the housekeeper, made it clear that his presence was a hindrance to her chores; he hadn't realised a sigh could communicate such ill feeling until the afternoon he walked across her freshly washed floor. Abel was looking forward to the midterm break at Halloween.

He stood at the sink washing his cup after a particularly irksome day, one of those days when the pupils buzzed a low hum of whispers and laughter despite his many stern looks and warnings; one of those days marking work when he seemed to write "did" or "have done" at least a dozen times; one of those days when he was just too tired to cope with James McCrea's constant pen tapping. He had erupted when he had explained the Maths exercise, the class had begun to put pencil to paper, and Eily Magee asked, "Sir, what page are we on?" He felt bad when she replied after his tirade, "Sorry, sir, I'll try to listen better." She was only a wee thing, and academia was never going to be her path in life. He had already drunk too much coffee during the day, but my God, could he use another cup to get through the rest of his work and drive home? After an hour, he gave up and began sliding books into his leather satchel and lining tomorrow's work up in straight, neat piles on his desk, setting the class register on top of the piles. He walked to the door, switched off the light, locked the door behind him and turned to leave when he heard it. The thud of footsteps across the old wooden floor in the schoolhouse. He stopped breathing. Listened. No, it must have been his imagination. He walked away. Thud, thud, thud. He turned back to the schoolhouse, opened the lock and flung open the door, flicking on the lights. The room was empty. Thud, thud, thud from the other side of the room divider. He threw that door to the wooden wall and flipped the light. Empty. From behind him, thud, thud, thud. He spun around. Silence. Thud, thud, thud behind his back, coming closer, louder. His feet refused to move. His mouth was dry. Silence. He turned slowly on the spot. There was no one there. Had the room been so cold? He could see his breath in the dull light. His fingers were little icicles. He breathed into his belly and slowly released his exhalation like he had been taught and strode to the back of the classroom, walked around the perimeter of the room, looked under desks, nothing. He switched off the light, closed the partitioned room door, and performed the same examination in the main school room. Nothing, no one. These old buildings could be creaky. The change of season was probably swelling the wooden beams and floorboards. Phantom noises that were no more than the schoolhouse adjusting to autumn. What silly thoughts he had for a fully grown man. He took his time closing and locking the schoolhouse—nothing to be afraid of. Driving away, he looked in the rearview mirror and, for just a second, saw the flicker of a flame in the tall windows. He blinked, and all was dark again.

At home, Abel ate some soup and dipped bread. He took out his phone to start searching for ideas to help wee Eily with her times tables, but the mobile phone reception inside the thick-walled cottage was even worse than in the village. He reminded himself to go to the library this week and use one of the computers there to order himself a laptop and printer. Something about Eily brought his mind to the girl in his old school. The day she'd come in with the bruised ear. Her mother's story that she fell off a swing. Always falling. He shook his head, rose, brought his dishes to the sink and washed them, scrubbed the kitchen, too, and put the guard tight around the smouldering fire. He bathed and went to bed early.

The next morning in school, he resolved to be more patient. Abel was determined to make progress with Eily Magee. After the roll, he set the children to copy and complete several pages of sums whilst he brought wee Eily to his desk. He explained that he was going to help her learn two multiplication facts each day and after a week, she would know all her five times tables. He started with five times one and patiently smiled at her when she replied, "One?" He was ready for this and brought out the little wooden cubes, laying five out on the desk for her to count. When she eventually gave the correct answer to five times one, he gave her a *Cola Cube* sweet with a huge smile that she shyly reciprocated. The rest of the day was just as satisfying, and he went home tired and fulfilled.

There was a definite chill in the air by now, and Abel lit the fire as soon as he arrived home. Once he had warmed up the little living room, he opened the door to let the rest of the heat spread through his home. There was no central heating in the cottage. In the only bedroom, an electric radiator was attached to the wall, but it didn't work, so the warmth from the fire would be his only source of heat. Still, the warmth of the cottage was not in its temperature but rather in the feeling of being home, safe, locked away from the world, in its three mismatched cups and thirteen plates of various colours and diameters, in the obtuse and acute angles of doorframes and windows, in the rivulet which streamed from the base of the tap into the old stone sink in the kitchen; the little house was perfect in its imperfections, made for Abel. That night, he slept long and deep.

By the time he arrived at the schoolhouse the next morning, a text message pinged on his phone: Róisín was sorry that she was sick and could not come in today. She hoped to be back tomorrow. He was irritated because he had planned more work with Eily Magee but supposed everyone was sick sometimes. Approaching winter, it was dark these mornings when he arrived at work. He unlocked the heavy door, which swung open by its own volition as was its wont. Flicking on the lights, Abel's eyes were drawn to the floor in the centre of the room. A puddle. He looked to the vaulted ceiling but could see no drips, it hadn't rained in a few days anyway. He gazed back at the puddle and saw more water. Foot-shaped puddles. From the leak in the centre of the floor, a set of wet footprints walked across the floor to his desk. He stepped across the floor, examining it for more water. He moved to the blackboard, back against the wall and looked again. One puddle and a straight line of footprints between it and his desk. He scrutinised it from every corner of the room. Where did the puddle come from, and how could footprints start in the middle of a room? He grabbed a ruler and laid it beside the first print, a full thirty centimetres. A man's footprint. Boots. Maybe someone had come in and walked through the puddle, the water creating the wet prints on the other side of it. But wasn't there only one set of keys? Wasn't there? It was then that he realised that the straight line of wet footprints traversed two rows of school desks, as if whoever had made the prints walked straight through the furniture. Abel spent so long trying to work out how the puddle and the man's footprints had appeared that before he knew it, the first pupils had begun to arrive.

"Good morning, Mr Keane," recited the three O'Neill siblings.

"Good morning, children. Grace, would you grab me the mop from the cupboard, please?" He asked the eldest child.

"What happened, sir?" she asked, hurrying to the cupboard.

"Just a leak," he replied.

"We've never had a leak here," she said as she began mopping.

"Is that so?" he answered, "I'll dry that up, Grace."

"It's ok, I don't mind helping, sir. Maybe you should light the stove, sir. We're foundered walking here in the cold."

"Good idea," he smiled.

The morning chugged along. It was neither a difficult day nor a fulfilling one; the pupils mostly did their work, not producing anything outstanding but not making trouble either. They seemed a little dulled by the cold. Although the stove roared, it didn't seem enough to heat the water for the cast iron radiators. Throughout the day, he moved from the stove to each of the radiators, rubbing the cold metal in the vain hope of some heat. The flames of the stove flickered in the faces of his young charges but did not raise the temperature in the room. After break time, Abel allowed the children to keep on their coats. By lunchtime, when the stove still hadn't warmed the room, and the radiators were still icy, he decided he would have to talk to the frugal priest about employing a plumber; otherwise, November in the classroom would be unbearable in the frigid schoolhouse. Remembering Fr Malachy's thriftiness, he closed the damper in the stove rather than waste more coal and let it smoulder to sleep. Being without an assistant, when the children left the schoolhouse, he was obliged to spend a few extra hours correcting the pupils' work. By six pm, the black windows appeared to be staring in on him. Pulling his coat tighter, lifting his car keys and empty coffee flask, he began to close up the schoolhouse. He dragged his fingers along the radiator at the doorway and pulled them back in surprise. His fingertips were roaring red. The radiator was boiling hot.

The sting in his fingertips each time he changed gear on the drive home brought back the crawling feeling on his neck. The radiators had not heated all day despite the lit fire. By the time he was leaving, there was only cold ash in the stove. When he discovered the hot radiator, he checked the other two heaters in the room and even went into the second classroom, they were all ice cold, and even the pipes which supplied them were cold. The puddle this morning, the wet footsteps through the desks. Something was not right about the schoolhouse.

He had no sooner closed the door in the cold cottage and set his things on the tiny dining table than his phone rang. Róisín calling to ask how he got on, to apologise for not being able for work today, and promising to be in tomorrow. As he told her about the day's lessons, Abel paced the living room and kitchen with the phone to one ear and tidied up with his free hand, lighting the fire and setting some soup on the hob to heat. She was concerned when he told her about the puddle.

"But we've never had a leak," she informed him.

"Yes, Grace O'Neill told me," he said.

She laughed when he told her about the warm radiator, "Sure, the stove doesn't even heat those radiators! There's an oil-fired boiler behind the schoolhouse, but…" she stopped.

"But what?" he asked.

"Fr Malachy let the tank run dry in April. I remember because we had a late snow, and the schoolhouse was so cold we had to close the school."

None of this made sense, but just at that second, he smelled his soup burning to the bottom of the old copper pot and quickly ended the call. Despite the unpleasant note of burnt potatoes, he ate quickly and cleaned up the kitchen. He opened the door from the living room into the kitchen to warm up the chilly room while he undressed for a bath; maybe he needed another early night. In the bath, he decided he would visit the priest tomorrow and insist on him employing a roofer to check for a leak in the roof and a plumber to fix the heating. He would take a look inside the oil tank himself first thing in the morning. Feeling some calm now that he had a plan, Abel lay in the bath reading until the water started to chill. In slippers and a dressing gown, he walked into the bedroom and stopped dead. The heat in the room was unbearable. On the broken radiator glowed a small red plastic light. The shimmering heat emanating from the radiator was enough to confirm the source of the heat. He pulled his phone from the dressing gown pocket and quickly snapped a photo. Without thinking twice, he sent the picture to Róisín with the words, *I did not switch this on – it has never worked!* He switched off the radiator and stared at his phone screen. Róisín had read the message immediately. After several minutes of watching the screen and waiting to read something other than *Róisín is typing*, he began to regret sending the photo. He was a teacher. For God's sake, she must think him crazy. His phone vibrated, *Weird! Talk tomorrow.* Ten minutes to type three words? She definitely thought he had a screw loose.

Arriving early at the schoolhouse, equipped with a short ladder and a flashlight, Abel peered into the hollow oil tank. It was completely empty except for stale fumes, a few leaves and what might once have been a mouse. There was nothing in here which could have fuelled a radiator. Róisín arrived earlier than usual and busied herself tidying the classroom and performing the few tasks Abel needed. He may have imagined it, but he felt she avoided eye contact. When he asked her a question, her answers were brief.

"You must think I'm mad," he suddenly said, "I was probably overtired yesterday dealing with the class alone."

"I'm sorry, I should have been here."

"Not at all, you couldn't help being sick," he replied.

"It was my mother's birthday," she said, "It's always a hard day."

Abel waited for her to explain. He listened as she told him about losing her parents when she was just fourteen years old. How Lynn, the priest's housekeeper, was her aunt and had looked after her. He felt bad; it had never occurred to him that she may have had things on her mind other than his unhinged notions. When she had finished, he said, "I'm sorry, I didn't know. If you need anything, just let me know."

"Thank you. Listen, we need to talk about what's been happening here." He looked at her and stared into her eyes. He had to admit the thought had crossed his mind too; she was a good-looking woman, they were of a similar age and neither of them married.

"I've noticed some things in the building too, but we'll talk after school; here comes Johnny Joe O'Donnell, running as usual," she said. He turned his red face to the worksheets on his desk.

By the time the last pupil had gone home, Róisín had everything ready for the next day's lessons. "He should really pay you for the full day, Róisín. You stay often enough," said Abel.

"Not at all, then I would have to stay all day or longer still; as it is, I stay when I want or when you really need me, but if he paid me for the full day, I'd have no choice in the matter," she replied.

"That makes sense, I suppose," he said, "So, what have you seen?"

"Oh, I haven't seen anything, but I've heard plenty," she said.

"What do you mean?"

"When I was assistant for Mr Jackson, your predecessor, I used to stay behind and clean and tidy up for him. He had been here for forty years or more and wasn't fit for it. He probably should have retired ten years before he did. To be honest, the children would have run rings around him if I'd let them, and he'd get a bit confused, so I used to set the work for him, but a kinder man you couldn't meet."

"You're very good."

"Well, I was until the footsteps."

"What do you mean?"

"It started one afternoon. I was here on my own, and I hadn't noticed how dark it had become. I decided it was time to go home when I heard this thud, thud, thud! Well, I fairly ran home after that. Then, it began to happen regularly. Thud, thud, thud. It was definitely the sound of a man walking across the floor, but there was never anyone else in the schoolhouse. Never happened during the day, only after dark. I gave the keys back to Mr Jackson and told him I couldn't stay after school anymore. I did what I could during the day, but in the end, Mr Jackson couldn't cope with the work and had to retire. I have never been here on my own after dark since then, and I won't be again."

Abel was silent. He said, "Did I tell you about me hearing footsteps too?"

"No, but after what you told me last night, I'm not surprised. And what about your radiator at home?"

"None of it makes any sense," he said.

"Do you believe in ghosts?" she asked.

He didn't know how to answer. Was she serious, or was she going to make fun of him? He didn't believe in ghosts, but lately… He had no explanation for the lit stove on his first day or for the appearance of the chalk sticks, for the footsteps, the puddle, the footprints, the radiators. Some of it he could attribute to the schoolhouse's old structure, but the radiator at home playing the same trick as that in the schoolhouse. It was as if someone, or something, was trying to make him take notice.

"I'm not sure," he answered.

"Me neither. To be honest, and don't you say a word of this to Fr McBride, but I'm not sure if I believe there is anything after this life at all. Still, there are some things I just cannot explain. When the footsteps started, I eventually confided in my aunt Lynn, and she had a theory. She told me about an old schoolmaster from before the schoolhouse was built."

"Go on."

"In the days of the Penal Laws, when Catholics weren't allowed to go to school, they went in secret to these hedge schools."

"Yes, I know, but what about it?"

"The old schoolmaster was Master McFaul. He'd take the lessons when it was safe, behind a hedge that would have been at the entrance to our schoolhouse. It's why the locals still call it The Hedge School. Teachers couldn't risk being caught, and Master McFaul was fastidious about his safety, so much so that he lived in a very unusual way. Just up the coast, years before, a boat had become wedged in a little enclave in the cliffs. The boat could only be reached at low tide or by climbing down a steep wee path from the top of the cliff. Master McFaul set himself up in the cabin of the old boat so that he wouldn't be caught off-guard. Teachers had to be secretive about their movements, and no one knew for a long time where he lived. When it was discovered, a local landowner, not agreeing with the laws, offered him one of his cottages, but the schoolmaster refused. It was certainly eccentric, but he was such a kind man to the children and their families that people accepted his quirk and let him be."

"That's an interesting story, but how is it related to the footsteps?"

"Master McFaul was a kind man, but he was no pushover. One day, one of the children came to his lessons and had clearly been beaten. It turned out his father had been too generous with the back of his hand. Well, Master McFaul was outraged, and after the children had gone, he went to the cottage of the bullying father. He warned him to keep his fists to himself, or he'd feel the back of Mr McFaul's own hand. That would have been the end of it. Except then, Master McFaul stopped coming to the hedge school. When they went to the boat to check on him, the locals found Master McFaul's beaten corpse in the boat cabin."

"I still don't see…"

"I'm getting there! A few days later, that bully of a father had sent the family out to find work and food. When they returned, the cottage was on fire. The father lay dead inside. But the children swore they saw the perpetrator walking away from the burning cottage.!

"It wasn't…?"

"Master McFaul," said Róisín.

Abel hadn't known how to respond. As he drove home, he asked himself how he was to believe that an angry schoolmaster's ghost was haunting the schoolhouse. He did not believe in the paranormal; like Róisín, he doubted there was anything after one died. He doubted, but he did not know. He also did not know what was happening at the schoolhouse. He was dog-tired. He had been trying so hard to make sense of what was happening, to reason with himself that there must be logical reasons for the illogical that he was utterly waned. He sat in the armchair beside the fireplace and pulled a throw over him, too exhausted to light a fire. He tried to keep his eyes open; his head was nodding and his chin dipping, his lower jaw falling open, starting him back to life. Burning. He could smell burning. He jumped up to go into the kitchen when he heard it. Click. He knew before he reached the kitchen door. On the floor. A stick of chalk. Broken in two. He stared at the pieces. And stared. He dared not take his eyes off them. He did not keep chalk in the house. He reached down to lift them off the floor. Something from the side of his eye. On the cold stone floor. Water. Footprints. As he straightened his back, he saw the set of footprints. Starting at the sink and ending in the centre of the kitchen floor.

"Jesus Christ!" he yelled.

He scooped up the broken chalk, grabbed a wad of kitchen paper, swiped away the footprints, and threw the whole lot in the waste bin. He muttered to himself as he pulled the curtains of every window in the cottage and climbed into bed. He opened the drawer beside the bed, reached to the back, and pulled out the little plastic bottle with a childproof cap, which he had kept just in case for the last four months, *Temazepam 10mg.* He swallowed two with water and lay back, waiting for the sleeping pills to pull him into blessed oblivion.

In his sleep, waves crashed on the blue-lit midnight beach. A ship rocked onto the shore. On the deck, a dark-cloaked figure stood unmoved by the tumbling of the boat. As the ship came closer to Abel, as it could only in dreams, he saw the wrinkled face of a man in clothes from centuries gone by. Under his left arm, he sheltered a girl. The girl. The girl Abel taught and whom he lost less than a year ago. The girl he could have saved if he'd only been taken seriously when he reported her bruises. She who would be alive if only the head teacher had not been afraid of her "good family"—her death which broke him. A cloud shrouded the moon, throwing the ship into obscurity till a single moonbeam lit up the girl's face. He could not make out what her lips were saying. He leaned in closer. Her face loomed in his. She screamed.

He opened his eyes. The bed was soaked with sweat. His damp forehead chilled quickly in the cold air. His heart was racing. His eyes, staring at the ceiling, were drawn to the bottom of the bedroom door. A shape moved across the slit of light. Light? There should be no light. The shape stopped. Two feet. The feet moved, walked away. Leaving just the glow at the bottom of the doorway. His body was heavy, but he willed himself out of the bed. His feet inched towards the door. What was on the other side? Abel turned the door handle slowly. The door creaked open and on the other side, nothing. Just the glow of the fire in the grate. He hadn't lit a fire. He stepped further into the room. The front door was ajar. On the rug in front of the hearth, two dark patches; on the stone floor, a set of wet footprints made their way out the front door. He ran back to the bedroom and dressed quickly. To this day, Abel could not explain why he left his house. What compelled him to drive to the schoolhouse in the middle of the night? He just knew he had to follow whatever had been in his home. Its footsteps had led the way out the door, but something in his heart drove him to the schoolhouse. It was the only other place in this village he knew.

The country road, unhindered by streetlights, was impossible to drive on at this time of night unless you were a local. Abel accelerated in stretches he knew from memory, braked at sharp bends, one step forward, two steps back. His feet stamped the floor as a pair of glowing amber eyes flashed at him. The fox sauntered off. Stared back at him as it slinked over the low dry-stone wall. A wave of fog rolled over the car as he started off again. He was driving blind. He exhaled slowly through his pursed lips, as he had been taught. Trying to steady his heart and calm the choppy breath in his lungs. He had to get to the schoolhouse. Why? He did not know, only that he must. Over the steering wheel, orange light began to break through the foggy shroud. He pulled out of the fog as if pulling off a blindfold. The schoolhouse was straight ahead. Flames tearing at the dark sky. He yanked the handbrake on and tumbled out of the car. He had to shield his eyes to look at the building; the light and heat were unbearable. Thud, thud, thud. Louder than he had ever heard it.

Thud, thud, thud, echoing off the cliffs and hills, filling the dark sky. Flames blinked and stared out of the high windows; thick smoke streamed from the schoolhouse door. He is flung against the car as something explodes, throwing roof tiles into the air landing all around him. Flames reach up into the night. Then he sees them. Two men. Grappling. Inside. He bounds forward. Stops. Something about the men, something not human, not any longer. The glass cracks, and fire grabs at the window frames. One man is all flames. He is made of fire. He slaps angrily at the other man. The other wraps one arm around the neck of the fiery man, and the other arm whips around the flaming torso. The flaming man recoils and pulls away. His opponent is water. Steam begins to escape the building. The two men lick, spit, twist, and wrestle in a storm of fire and rain. The schoolhouse is a cacophony of cracks, hisses, bangs and shudders. Abel covers his ears. The flames die, and the light dims. Smoke and steam fill the little hedgy enclave. The roofless, glassless schoolhouse smoulders. The doors stand wide open. Out steps a man, the watery man. Water no more. A real, solid man. Apart from his clothing. Abel knew then. The schoolmaster. He walked past Abel and melted into the night. As Abel turned to watch him go, in front of him, shivered a little girl. The little girl.

"Mr Keane, are you ok?"

He recognised the voice first, "Eily, what are you doing out here?"

"I saw the fire, sir."

"How, Eily? Your house is away up the road."

The girl looked at her feet. So did Abel. She was barefoot.

"Eily?"

The girl said nothing. He opened the car door and lifted her inside. In the car light, he saw her left eye swollen. He got into the driver's seat and said, "Eily, you can tell me. You can tell me anything at all. I'll do everything that I can to help."

And she did. He had to use every ounce of self-restraint he possessed not to drive straight to Eily's father's house and beat the bastard to a pulp.

No, this girl he would save. No mistakes this time.

MILK HOUSE

I t might be a comforting idea that life prevails after death, but I did not believe in ghosts. I had never seen one. There were no credible photographs of ghosts. No one I knew had ever had a definite encounter with someone from the other side. In the deepest pits of grief, no one had spoken to me softly from the beyond to say, "It's ok; I'm still here."

So, I defied shadowy shapes in dark corners, creaking sounds in unoccupied rooms, prickling neck hair whilst walking to the bathroom in the quiet of the night, fearsome seconds between walking into a dark room and switching on lights and feeling that there is someone there when there is no one there. Being able to shrug off fears of the bogeyman was a blessing when I needed to be alone to recover from the loud, hectic, exhausting business of people.

People of my generation still talk about that winter in the same way that my father used to tell me stories of The Big Freeze of 1963. Seasons here tend to merge into a murky thing. A few days of uninterrupted sunshine in summer is a heatwave, and it barely takes an inch of snow to snow us in. But that winter was harsh. The snow started in fits in November, building until the eventual thaw in late January, with a few stubborn spells of heavy snowfall well into late spring. During the worst weeks, flights were cancelled, whole flocks of sheep froze to death on hills wrapped in snow drifts, water pipes froze, electricity lines sagged and snapped under the weight of huge icicles, and vehicles spun out of control and into ditches on the few roads that were considered passable.

An unfamiliar light girdling my bedroom window woke me the first morning. I pulled back the curtains to reveal a world encased in bright, brilliant snow. I moved from one window to the next, checking; all around was completely, utterly covered. There comes a point in winter when it seems like darkness has won, and there will never again be more than a couple hours of dim daylight, but the gleaming snow was a shiny nod of encouragement.

Downstairs, I spooned ground coffee into the funnel of the moka pot, replaced it into the base and screwed on the pot, setting it on the stove and lighting the gas before I made for the back door to bring in Biddie from her kennel in the outhouse. Pulling a woolly hat over my hair, I unlocked the door and jumped back just in time to avoid a small avalanche of snow burying my slippered feet. As well as the tumbling loose snow, my exit was blocked by more than a foot of the stuff. Climbing over the uneven white mounds, I managed not to fall. Pulling back the bolt on the door of the outhouse and pushing it open, Biddie stepped from her kennel with eyes half open, yawned, and stretched her front paws on my legs before licking my wrist and bounding out into the garden. She ran and bounced in circles, sniffing at the unfamiliar terrain and lifting her head to bark towards the sky before squatting to leave a small yellow circle in the snow.

Indoors, an icy puddle replaced the snow that had toppled in. Cold, bright light filled the house. The coffee pot spluttered, hissed, and warmed the house with its velvet scent. I poured coffee into a chipped mug, adding milk and two teaspoons of sugar. Biddie reached her paws onto my knee, elongating her small body, and reminded me with a gentle scratch on my leg that she was hungry. I filled her bowl with some leftover chicken and topped it up with brown pellets of dog food. As she crunched and snorted her way through her breakfast, I walked through the rooms of the house. Located on the side of one of the hills which ringed the city, straddling the cusp of urban and rural, the house had never-ending views: the industrial landscape of the city docks, square miles of suburban houses, schools and churches, fir tree forests and fields between the peaks which circled the city. Today, all was white.

Ten years ago, when I finally managed to make a living from writing, I decided to buy my first house. Originally the dwelling on a tiny dairy farm, the house had been built just before the turn of the last century. I had spotted it online after weeks of searching and decided it was mine. Bigger than the apartments I had been renting since university, close to the city but sitting in an acre field, the house, Milk House, according to the estate agent's website, seemed perfect.

Striding through the half-door of the house for the first time, however, my nostrils revolted at the smell of damp and mould. Ominous patterns of black spots grew from floor to ceiling on every wall; the floors creaked, and some boards had crumbled away; in the mottled green living room stood the last occupants' furniture, the style suggesting they had been gone quite some time. The kitchen consisted of two heavy free-standing cabinets filled with sticky crockery, a jaw box sink, and an ancient stove. There was an unfurnished room to the front, which might have housed livestock at one time, judging by the smell. Access to the upper floor was by a staircase, more like a ladder, several of the treads lying in powdery heaps on the floor below, the remaining steps ready to join them. The three bedrooms and bathroom were divided by walls almost a foot thick. A tarnished metal bedstead stood in the middle of a huge, patterned rug in the largest bedroom. Beside the bed, on the rug, was a rusty brown stain three feet long. In another room, through the windowpane, was growing a tree branch, a third of the way into the room. With slumped shoulders, I realised why this apparent gem had been affordable - who would buy this millstone of a house? Leaving, I slowly pulled the door closed, took a few steps back and looked up at the whole façade of Milk House.

Over the next few days, however, my mind kept coming back to Milk House; I could not afford to do the work, but my mind wouldn't let it go. I pictured log fires in the large stone fireplace and yearned for isolation amongst the trees on the hill. When the estate agent rang a fortnight later to say that the price had dropped, it seemed fate had stepped in. Within eight weeks, the house belonged to me. Three months followed of plans, discussions, building work, repairs, replacements and restoration. With the builders finally gone and the last screw turned, I looked around my house and smiled. I was home.

Even after so long, I still walked around the house for no reason other than to marvel that it was mine, that I made this, awed yet by the ever-changing scenery through the windows of the rooms of Milk House. Other than a few flurries, I had never seen a proper snowfall like this at the house. The snow hushed the city noises and all around was bright, shining and clean. Hugging my coffee in both hands, I grinned as I drank down the realisation that I was cut off from everyone and everything below.

I spent the first few hours of the morning writing with Biddie curled up on my feet, but every so often, distracted, I stood up and looked out one of the windows at the perfect white ground and the fast-falling snow; it was becoming deeper. I decided to heat some soup for lunch, but after a minute or two on the old stove, the gas flame petered and disappeared. Walking to the gas boiler housed under the stairs, I heard it roaring furiously; opening the cupboard door, I switched the boiler off for fear it might explode and made my way through the back door, through the blizzard, to the external wall behind the boiler. Through snowflake-laden eyelashes, I located the pipes and stared a while before realising that I had no idea what purpose any of them served. I hurried back indoors and shook off the snow at the back door.

"Just a sandwich for lunch today then, Biddie," I said, and she cocked her head and pricked her ears.

After a chilly lunch of cold chicken between two slices of almost stale bread, in the living room, I lit the fire in the stone fireplace, pulled an armchair closer to the burgeoning flames and opened the uninspiring novel I had been reading on and off for the last month. Other than bringing in Biddie that morning and my musings on the workings of the boiler, I had not been outdoors. I never liked to be the first to disturb a new snowfall; it was like destroying a piece of art. Trying to remember which character was which, I looked up at the window facing the fireplace. Although not much after 3pm., the light was already dimming, the scenery taking on a bluish hue. Deciding to put on a jumper, I rose and again looked through the windows at the unspoilt visage in front of my house; the streetlamps and houses below were beginning to light up, and the snow had eased to a gentle but steady fall. Biddie followed at my feet as I climbed the stairs and went into the bedroom to get a jumper. Given the boiler's failure, the house beyond the living room was cold; thankfully, the chimney that the bedroom shared with the fireplace in the room below would eventually warm the room a little, but I placed an extra blanket on the bed and closed the curtains tightly on the frigid view. As I turned to leave the room, from underneath the newly laid blanket, Biddie looked up at me out of lowered eyelids.

"Come on, Biddie, you are not sleeping there!" She followed at heel with her head slunk.

I do not watch much television, so I spent the evening in front of the fireplace with a glass of Malbec, trying to get back into the paperback, from time to time throwing a log on the fire and poking it to watch the patterns that the flames and embers made. I had not made much progress in my writing today but no matter, I would have plenty of time to work tomorrow; besides, with Biddie curled on my lap, I could hardly bear to abandon her for my desk on such a bitter night. Around midnight, I began my fastidious routine of switching off all plugs and removing them from the sockets, checking all the doors and downstairs windows, despite not having opened a window in weeks. I placed the heavy fireguard on the hearth and ensured it was secure around the dying fire. Deciding the outhouse would be too cold, I dragged Biddie's chewed-up bed close to the fire and beckoned her to use the great outdoors bathroom. She followed me through the kitchen to the back door but when I unlocked it, she stood stock still. I whistled, clapped my hands, clicked my tongue and walked out the door backwards, calling her out. With a lowered head, she crept towards me, squatted quickly in the snow, and then scrambled back indoors. I relocked the kitchen door and checked the handle and bolts. Biddie was already in her bed in front of the fire, not daring to catch my eye in case I changed my mind and forsook her to her kennel. I smiled, "Goodnight, Biddie."

The Malbec had taken hold quickly and I fell asleep within minutes of climbing into bed but awoke after a few hours with a dripping nose and icy feet. The little heat conducted by the fire in the hearth below had dissipated, and my breath misted in the air in front of my face. After an eternity of shifting around in bed, pulling blankets around me against the arctic draught, raising my knees to my chest and rubbing my cold feet with hands not much warmer, I got out of bed, put my feet into slippers and threw the blanket around my shoulders. The house seemed quieter than usual as I descended the stairs. I peeked into the living room at Biddie curled into a croissant shape which only dogs can achieve. Checking it was full, I plugged in the electric kettle and boiled water. A boiling kettle seems unnaturally loud in the dead of night. I lifted a box of cereal and read the ingredients. When the water had boiled, I placed a teabag into a cup, filled it and added milk, leaving the teabag in the cup. Leaning against the sink and holding the steaming mug close, I lifted the cereal box and continued my distracted read. My heart thumped in my chest.

"You."

Just one word. I spun and looked behind me. Nothing. I tilted my head and listened. Nothing. I crept back to the living room. The door was tightly shut. No sound. My heart pounded. Throwing open the door of the living room, Biddie leapt from her bed, howling and running around in circles. I switched on the light and scanned the room, looking into every corner. Nothing. No one. The mind plays tricks in the quiet.

"Shush, girl, it's ok," I told Biddie and myself as I scooped her up in my arms, quickly switching off the lights and pulling the doors shut before taking the stairs two at a time and abandoning my tea wherever I had left it. Biddie slept in the bend of my belly under the blankets that night.

Biddie woke me the next morning, licking my chin and nudging her snout under my elbow. I groaned as I got out of bed, feeling a lot stiffer than I should. Realising that she probably needed to relieve herself, I hurried downstairs, unlocked the kitchen door and put Biddie outdoors. The snow at the door was much higher than yesterday but barely fell in through the door, compacted by its own weight. I left her outside and used the toilet myself before opening the curtains throughout the house. The brilliance shone through the house, and I laughed at my childishness during the night. At least Biddie had enjoyed a spoiling as a result of my wine-addled imagination. After feeding the dog and drinking some instant coffee, I showered, determined not to be distracted by a drop of snow and to write at least a chapter today. I lit the fire and brought my laptop to the armchair next to it. With no gas, I was reliant on the heat of the fire and would have to go outside to replenish the logs and coal. I carried two wicker baskets to Biddie's outhouse behind the house, where I kept the logs. The bolt on the outhouse door was melded with ice. I hurried indoors to fetch some lukewarm water to defrost the bolt, remembering from somewhere not to pour boiling water on frozen metal for fear of it snapping. After thirty minutes of defrosting and trips between the outhouse and the house laden with baskets of logs, my job was done. For no reason other than the fact that it had been there when I bought the house, I kept coal in an old bunker at the bottom of the pathway that led to my front door. Steeling myself for the icy trek through the snow, I opened the front door for the first time in two days. Biddie, always at my feet, sat rigid as the cold air blew in on her face. I reached down to ruffle the fur on her neck. Turning around to start my slog, I stopped dead.

Leading to my front door, stopping an inch from it, was a single set of deep footprints. I slammed the door and swivelled around, the living room blurring. I searched my brain, had I left the house and forgotten? I scraped the door open again—one set of footprints pointing towards the door. I turned my head and scanned the snow all around. A blanket of crisp, undisturbed snow. One set of footprints deep in the snow, no others. I closed the door, bolted it and stepped backwards. I could not work it out. I had definitely not left the cottage since before the snow had begun.

Had someone called at the house? Who would have called? When could they have called? It was a small cottage; why did I not hear them? Why had Biddie not barked? I opened the door again. If someone had come to the door and knocked in vain, where were the footprints leading away from the house? A thought grabbed me. I slammed the door, bolted it and bound upstairs to my bedroom. Had someone come to the house and, thinking no one was at home, climbed to the upper floor to gain entry? The window in my bedroom above the front door was shut and locked, as it was when I had gone to bed the previous night. I quickly checked all the windows upstairs, shut and locked. The back door flashed in my mind. I had left it open as I fetched logs from the outhouse. I leapt down the stairs and ran to the back door. Shut and bolted. I checked the windows downstairs; all the same. I searched the floor around the front door for footprints, surely wet from snowy feet; nothing. I stared at the front door. Biddie stared at me, head tilted. Unbolting and opening the front door to the house, I stretched my head out and turned it to inspect the ground around the perimeter of the house; it was untouched. I looked again at the single set of footprints leading to my front door, pushed the door closed and bolted it.

The rest of the day, I turned the footprints over in my head. Finally, I told myself that they must have been the result of some sort of natural phenomenon; perhaps the footprints were the impression of my own well-worn steps to the house. That made more sense than the alternative. After checking the few storage closets that were in the house, just in case, I returned to the kitchen, refilled the kettle and switched it on. Looking in the refrigerator, I realised that I had not been prepared to be snowed in; apart from a spongey onion and a red pepper, which had left a little pile of pink goo on the bottom shelf of the fridge when I lifted it, there was the remainder of the chicken I had cooked a few nights ago and some ham in a packet marked with a use-by date for today. The bread had grown greenish-blue furry spots, which I might be able to slice off, and the jug of milk was running low. I took some of the ham and chicken into the living room along with two slices of bread, mouldy crusts removed, and toasted the bread on the fire, reasoning that the flames would kill anything untoward. As I ate, Biddie sat on her bed with her hind legs tucked under her body, waiting for some scraps. I never could say no to those pleading brown eyes, so despite the inadequacy of my own meal, I saved her a morsel of chicken and rewarded her patience with the last of my lunch, a pat on the head and a "good girl."

Moving to leave it back in the kitchen, the plate dropped out of my hand. Behind my armchair, in the kitchen doorway, stood the jug of milk. A taste of metal flashed on my tongue. Rooted where I stood, sweat cooled on my forehead. Inhaling deeply, I moved towards the milk jug. I bent my knees and reached for the jug, looking around and above my head. I touched the jug and snatched my hand away as a jolt shot up my arm to my shoulder. I reached again for the jug and lifted it by its handle. It was full of milk. Frozen solid milk.

My mind spun. Who did this? Who was in the house? Where had they hidden? Where were they now? My eyes were transfixed on the jug in the doorway, unwilling to see who had placed it there. Lifting my head quickly, I looked around the living room. Another blizzard at the window made it seem like the house was being thrown around inside a dense snow cloud. Taking a deep breath, I edged towards the kitchen doorway. Looking around for something to use as a weapon, I spotted the cast iron poker and lifted it as quickly and quietly as I could, never moving my eyes from the doorway. Taking several deep, slow breaths to try and ease my trembling limbs, I moved towards the doorway. Placing my left foot on a loose floorboard, it creaked, and I swung the poker about wildly, stabbing at the empty air. I hurdled from room to room, waving the poker all about me and stabbing at every sudden noise. Finishing the search in my bedroom, out of breath, I shouted, "Get out, this is private property!"

Looking at the poker in my hand, I added, "And I'm armed."

"You."

That single word again. I swallowed.

"Get out!" I shouted, louder this time, the pitch higher. I faltered. Should I go downstairs again? Blindly chase this intruder out of my house? A screeching yelp slashed at my ears. Bile filed my mouth; I ran downstairs. The living room was in near darkness. I couldn't see Biddie.

"Biddie! Where are you?" I shouted.

I plugged in a lamp and clicked the switch, but nothing happened. The bulb must have blown. I tried another, no good. Sliding my hand in my pocket, I pulled out my phone, flicking on the torch, I noticed no Wi-Fi signal. A wave of cold ran down my neck; the electricity must be out. I shone the light into the corners of the room; no sign of Biddie. Stepping around the jug of milk, I moved into the kitchen and shone the light across the floor. Where was she? I called out again, "Biddie, come on, girl, where are you?"

I stood still and steadied my breath, listening for her, straining my ears. Hearing heavy panting, I followed the sound back into the living room. Again, I tracked the beams of the torch around the room but could see nothing; hearing only the panting, I crouched to the floor, and the sound became louder; shining the light along the floor, I spotted a movement under the armchair. I moved closer and reached out. Biddie had not hidden under the armchair since she was a nervous puppy. What had happened to scare her?

"It's ok, Biddie, come on out," I said, swallowing the lump in my throat.

I could sense fear in the panting and stretched my hand further under the chair to coax her out. Feeling the hot moisture of breath on the back of my hand, I felt about in the darkness under the chair when there came a clattering on the staircase, and Biddie sprang through the door, barking wildly and running towards me. I pulled back my hand from under the chair and snatched Biddie into my arms. Blood pulsed in my ears as I jumped to the other side of the room with Biddie clinging to me, her claws scratching my arms. If not Biddie, what was under the chair? I stood staring at the chair for a long time, resisting the urge to run out the front door. I had heard the panting and felt the breath on my hand, but if Biddie was upstairs, what was under the chair? Balancing Biddie under one arm and pointing the phone torch, I rushed across the room and pulled the chair away. A spider dashed from the torch beam, and a few balls of dust and dog hair tumbled, but nothing else appeared. I exhaled slowly.

Sitting down, stroking Biddie's head, the beating blood in my ears slowed, and I tried to understand. Seeing the snow now approaching the height of the windowsills, it was clear that the failure of the gas and electricity was due to the weather. What had been panting under the chair? How and why had the milk jug been refilled, frozen and moved? What I had told myself about the footprints was nonsense. The word *you* reverberated inside my head. And the yelp, did Biddie even make that noise? What had scared or hurt the dog, and why could I not find her when I searched?

Exhausted, I threw more logs onto the fire and walked slowly to the stairs to retrieve blankets and jumpers; with no electricity or gas, I would be confined to the living room for heat and light, although the latter was fading fast. On my way back downstairs, passing the boiler cupboard under the stairs, I added a box of candles to my supplies. Maybe I should try and get away from the house, but where would I go; the cottage was half a mile from the nearest house, not a big distance, but the hill was steep and I had never seen such deep snow. It was nearly dark, and what would I say, even if I didn't break both legs in the trek down the hill to my nearest neighbours, whom I'd never seen or uttered a word to? *There have been some noises and things moving in my house.*

I would hole up in the living room and keep warm beside the fire; maybe the snow would stop by the following morning, maybe even thaw, and I could make my way downhill for help. This was ridiculous. I was hungry and overtired, had been alone too long and had imagined things. There was nothing in my house that a hot meal, light and heat wouldn't sort out. With renewed hope, I tried switching on the boiler again, but of course, with no electrical supply, it did nothing. I stopped in the kitchen and looked in the fridge; it was still cold and still bare. I put the remaining chicken and ham in my mouth and finished the meat in a couple of gulps. Pouring some dry food into her bowl, I called for Biddie. I was greeted with a low growling.

Returning to the living room, I looked at Biddie. She was standing on the settee staring at the window, snarling a noise I had never heard her make, a ridge of hair spiking from her neck to her tail. I moved closer. Ice rippled from the top of my head down my body. At the window stood a man. His eyes looked at me, and through me, his face was stony. I was fixed to the spot. Something did not fit. He was dressed in trousers, a woollen jacket, and a flat cap, like an old man, but he did not look any older than thirty. His eyes, his skin and his clothes were different shades of an icy grey.

"Who are…" I started as he began to raise his hand from his side.

"You."

My ears rang, hearing the word in the distance, "You." My feet were stuck to the floor, but my knees swivelled. Biddie stopped growling and came to my side. The grey figure raised his hands and touched the glass of the window.

"You," it said.

His grey fingertips rested on the window pane. He moved forward. I jumped back. His fingers pressed the glass and began to glide through it. I could not be seeing what I was seeing. Inch by inch, the grey figure slithered into the room. Never breaking eye contact, it moved closer and closer to me. I opened my mouth, but it was dry, and no sound came out. Sweating, I broke his stare and snatched up Biddie. Bolting to the front door, I tore it open and scrambled over the wall of snow. The footprints were gone. I battled to get away. A memory of trying to run through sea waves sparked in my head. Still, I hauled one leg after the other as quickly as I could. I wanted to look back but couldn't. I didn't want to know if the grey man was upon me. Falling face first into the snow, Biddie leapt from my arms, racing ahead. She barked furiously and circled back. I followed as best I could with feet that were heavy and numb. Seeing the heavy wooden farm gate ahead, I ploughed on. The gate, half covered, was wedged closed in the snow. Biddie jumped through the upper slats and turned towards me, howling at me from the other side. I reached the gate and pulled myself up, but I couldn't feel my feet or work my legs. I launched myself at the gate, caught hold of the slat and lugged myself towards it. I threw one leg over the top and turned to look back at the house. I heard a crack and saw the branches overhanging the gate move in a slow arc as I fell to the ground.

I awoke with a jolt and stared at a mustard, tasselled lampshade beside my head. A pink blanket was tucked up under my chin. Turning my head, pain shot the back of my eyes. Biddie sat on a rug in front of an open fire by the trainer-clad feet of a teenage boy and an elderly woman. The woman rose and pulled her mauve cardigan tightly around herself. Her knitwear suited her blue-rinsed hair. Biddie jumped up and nudged herself under my arm.

"Daniel, here…" began the old woman.

The boy interrupted, "It's Dan, actually."

"*Dan* found you knocked out in the snow and brought you down here," continued the old woman.

"Thank you, Dan," I said.

For the next few minutes, my head whirled with the old woman, Mrs Palmer, and her grandson Dan talking over each other and filling me in on my rescue. As they chattered, I noticed a damp feeling between my legs and hoped it was from running in the snow and not anything else. My right ankle throbbed, too.

Mrs Palmer rested her hand on my knee and asked, "So what happened?"

"I'm not sure. It sounds silly… there was someone, or something, in my house," I said.

"Where's your house?" Dan asked.

"Milk House," I replied.

The old woman and Dan looked at each other. Dan's eyes widened, but Mrs Palmer smiled gently and told me to tell her everything. After a faltering start and a reddening face, I told the boy and his grandmother my story, which I wasn't sure I believed myself. When I had finished, I looked down at Biddie, not daring to meet their eyes. Dan was silent, maybe a little paler than when I had begun.

"You know," said Mrs Palmer, "that house was built on a wee dairy farm. That's how it got its name, although we rarely called it that. My uncle Peter owned it when I was just a girl. He only had a handful of cows; the farmland was too hilly for grazing, but he sold every last ounce of milk he got out of those cows. He had a horse and cart, even in the '60s, and sold the milk himself, mostly to friends and family, mind you. Anyway, in 1962, Peter married my aunt and brought her to the house. Before long, she was expecting a baby and the two of them were as happy together as you've ever seen two people. Peter worked hard. I doubt there was much money in the little milk he produced, but he was up and down that hill in his horse and cart, selling every drop in all weather.

"The Big Freeze came in 1963; we'd never seen snow like it. People didn't go about in cars much then, so they got about alright in the snow on foot. Of course, his house was up on the hill, and Peter needed to use the cart to carry his milk and he wouldn't let people down either. My aunt was nearing her time when Peter went out one morning and didn't come back. No one knew she was up there alone, though; we had no phones in those days. At the end of his round, his old horse collapsed in the snow on the other side of the city. He had to abandon the cart and walk. Normally, he could've done it in a couple of hours, but it took him half the day with the snow five feet high.

"As soon as he arrived home, he knew something was wrong. His old dog was cowering when he came through the door, and his wife was nowhere to be seen."

Mrs Palmer removed her glasses and wiped her eye with a tissue she pulled from the sleeve of her cardigan.

"He found them both in the bed upstairs. Her and the baby. It had come early, too early. He came down here in a terrible state to fetch my mother, but there was nothing she could do. It was too late. She had bled heavily. My mother never got over the sight, the blood and both of them ice cold."

The boy stared at the floor, biting the corner of his lip.

"He never remarried. Stayed up there alone till he died himself. I always thought it strange."

"What do you mean?" I asked.

"It was twenty years before we saw another snow, anything like that, and when we did, he passed too."

I had the feeling that what I was hearing, I'd heard before, and I already knew the answer to my question.

"What was her name?"

"She was Auntie Eugenia, but Peter always called her Eu."

THE CHAPEL IN SANVICCI

The light on the Côte d'Azur, the blues of the sky swimming perfectly into the sea. As the train speeds in and out of long dark tunnels, white beaches full of coloured parasols float past. Through the opposite train window, great green mountains slip into the sea. Saint-Tropez, Cannes, Juan-les-Pins, Antibes, Nice, Monaco; days on the beach, late lunches, later dinners, cocktails, tanned bodies, money, parties, haute couture, a little bit of the nineteen-twenties, still swinging – all glimpsed through gaps in the trees that line the railroad.

Standing with his arm leaning on an open window in the corridor, a young man scribbles in a notebook. His eyebrows are knitted together, and huge headphones keep the outside out. He wears a dark *Ramones* tee shirt. His jean shorts are hacked off at the knee. Black socks bunch up about the top of oxblood *Doctor Marten* boots. I wonder what he writes in his little notebook. Wonder about his use of paper in this digital age. Maybe he is trying to put his first love into words. He might be on some journey of self-discovery through the countryside, substituting the SNCF train for a failing motorcycle, meeting authentic locals and planning a revolution. Gazing at his notebook, it takes me a while to realise that he is looking back at me. I turn my head and stare at the blackness beyond the window of the tunnelled train.

Hypnotised by the gentle bouncing of the train along the tracks, I must have fallen asleep. I was wakened, slack-jawed and dry-mouthed by a young blonde woman dragging her suitcase across my knees. I would normally have offered to help her, but she seemed so put out by my being there that I swung my legs to the side and looked the other way. I doubted her muttered "Salaud" was a compliment. The young writer was gone. I pulled my own suitcase from the rack above my head and left the compartment to make my way out of the station and onwards to my hotel.

Sanvicci is one of the first towns on the journey into the Italian Riviera. The taxi bounced along the cobbled streets, and more than once, I shut my eyes, certain that the cab was about to collide with a *Vespa* or a reversing lorry. We passed designer shops shoed into the bottom floor of creamy crumbling buildings, cafes with tables jutting onto the roads, here and there, a washing line was strung between buildings in narrow streets, brilliant white clothing like bunting. The driver stopped outside the *L'Abbazia* hotel, repeated something in Italian a few times and gestured with his hands at the hotel sign. Under huge yellow awnings on either side of the entrance, black-shirted waiters served coffee and cold drinks to guests sitting at cast iron tables. I paid the driver when he set the case down; he shook my hand, leapt back into the taxi and vanished.

After check-in, I was shown to my room and left alone. The room was on the third floor and well air-conditioned. The old-fashioned furniture and décor was chic in the Italian way. Facing the bed were tall glass doors onto a small balcony. I stepped out into the close heat and shielded my eyes to take in the view. Far beyond the stepping stones of buildings, past the abandoned rail track, was the famous azure of the sea. To my left, a shopping district bustled, shops with names found in fashion magazines, glass-fronted and minimalist, little cafes with overpriced coffee, the rich and beautiful idling by, wearing oversized sunglasses and carrying shopping bags from shops of the *Chanel* variety. Directly to my right was an old church, La Cappella di Santa Fina. The elevated chapel was reached by two curved sets of steps which flowed from either side of the ornate wooden doors down to the street below. Below, in the semicircle formed by the steps, stood a statue, presumably of Santa Fina, with flowers at her feet. Beyond the church stood a huge white building with an ascending path carving its way through orange and purple blossoming gardens up to a lavish façade. Above the three double doors was the pink neon word *Casinò*.

I unpacked the few things I had brought, placing the box in the bedside table drawer, pushing it behind the *Gideon* bible and closing the drawer tight. In the tiny windowless bathroom, I showered, washing off the grime of the long journey. I dressed, folded a few euros into my pocket, and left my room. Too early for dinner, I sat at a table close to the hotel entrance and ordered un caffè.

Locals strolled along, enticing and ignoring the attention of the seated onlookers. A little dark-haired boy dressed in tan and white chased pigeons from the cast iron tables to the cobblestones and back. I wondered what he would do if he caught one. I must have sat there for a long time because the sun was no longer reflected off the whitewashed walls of the street when the waiter smiled and looked at me, asking if I wanted another coffee. Instead, I signed the palm of my hand with an imaginary pen and said, "Per favore."

I wandered down through the town towards the sea, crossing the disused train tracks and the train station converted into a row of little shops. That the new railroad ended at an underground station in Sanvicci seemed apt. Along the promenade, Italian families and tourists headed away from the beach as the sun slipped into the sea. I had hoped for a vivid sunset, but a cloudless day brings only a dull dusk.

When the last of the sun had seeped from the sky and the air had lost some of its heat, I walked back towards my hotel. On the way, I ate a pizza slice bought from a window in the wall of a local pizzeria. On the hill, the white stucco casino was lit by floodlights, and the neon sign shone brightly against the dark sky. Vaguely familiar pop music bubbled from somewhere as I returned to my room. I sat in a chair by the window and looked out at the casino; men in dinner jackets and women in long dresses floated in and out of the golden light of the huge doorways. Families walked along the street below, wondering at the glamour of it all. Beside me on a little round table was a complimentary bottle of wine labelled *Rossese di Dolceacqua*. I'd never heard of it, but needing a drink, I uncorked the bottle and filled one of the two wine glasses on the table. Sitting in the darkening room, staring at the illuminated town, I sipped steadily from the glass.

The crowds below swelled and shrank, cafes filled and emptied, lights shone and dimmed, and my wine bottle slowly emptied. As night slipped into early morning, I dozed on and off in the chair by the window. The casino did not sleep, a steady ebb and flow of glamorous gamblers, noiseless in the distance.

We had met at the casino in Monte Carlo eight years ago, not inside the casino but nervously hanging around the huge doors, peeking in at the exhibition of outrageous wealth indoors. We locked eyes, laughed at our awkwardness, and went our separate ways. Later, her auburn, almost maroon, hair appeared in front of me in a queue for ice cream close to the *Café de Paris*. I touched her shoulder and reddened deeply when her surprise turned to laughter as I stammered, "We have to stop meeting like this." I don't remember much of the rest of that night or how we began to spend the next seven years together; in a way, there was no beginning. Once I knew Therese, I had always known her.

A flutter of red silk below the statue of Santa Fina pulled me out of my memories. At the foot of the statue clung a woman who could have been thirty years old or fifty. In her hand, she held the straps of a pair of red stilettos. Her silk dress draped diagonally from her right shoulder down to her left thigh. Her tightly curled head was bent as if in prayer. Pulling my chair closer to the doors, she turned to look up at me, showing mascara-stained cheeks. She let go of the statue and moved to the steps, ascending barefoot to the doors of the church. She put her hand to the ornate wooden door, and turned again, locked eyes with me and held my stare as she slipped into the church and closed the door silently behind her. I don't know what drove me to my door, down the hotel stairs, through the lobby and up the church steps. After running up the church steps, I grabbed at the door handle and tried to turn it. No movement. I twisted my hand, but it just slid over the grooves of the handle. I put my left hand over my right and tried again. Locked tight. I stepped back and looked around me.

No one to be seen. I looked up at my room, glass doors still open, the neck of the wine bottle just about visible. I descended the steps and looked around for another door but could see none. I stood at the statue of Santa Fina and looked up at the church. In a gap between the peak of the church roof and the casino, I could see a terracotta roof; the church was connected to another building behind it, perhaps a monastery or a convent. The woman in red must have entered that building via the church and locked the church door behind her. I sauntered a few metres back towards my hotel and glanced up at my room.

I looked again. In the glass door was the reflection of the woman. Bounding back to my room, I passed the night manager and took the stairs two at a time. I swiped the key card three times before the little green light illuminated. I swung the door open and stared at an empty room. The tiny bathroom, too, was empty. I pulled open the wardrobe doors, nothing but my few clothes. On my hands and knees, I looked under the bed. I sank back into the chair by the window, breathless. I started from the church back to my room. Wiping cold sweat from my forehead, I smirked doubtfully at my stupidity: too much wine and not enough sleep, chasing phantom women at dawn.

I stripped, filled an unused wine glass with water from the sink in the bathroom, probably not drinkable, sat down on the bed, opened the drawer, took a single pill from the box behind the bible, swallowed it with a gulp of water and lay down, pulling a single sheet over me. I slept until nearly 1pm.

After lunch at the hotel, I wandered through the town, fleeting glimpses into shops selling clothes I could neither afford nor ever wear. Some of the smaller shops were closed, their workers taking temporary refuge from the intense afternoon heat. Perfumed, refrigerated air blasted from the plate glass boutiques, passers-by pausing in relief. I arrived at the hotel where Therese and I had honeymooned.

Hotel Marie-Antoinette had once been a huge family villa, now converted into an overly expensive hotel, five storeys high, pastel pink, adorned with balustraded windows and cake icing plaster curlicues. Overlooking the beach, its terrace stretched into the sea, rows of tanned bodies on sun loungers perusing the beach bathers below, parasol-shaded tables leading back to the hotel's French doors. We had sipped pinot grigio, leaning into each other and giggling at the smiling automatic "Buongiorno' or "Buona sera" that tripped off staff's tongues on sighting a guest, regardless of their current pursuits. Therese had pointed out a receptionist gesticulating wildly and spewing a barrage of angry Italian words at the hotel gardener seconds before both staff turned to an elderly American couple, grinning "Buona sera, Signora Tyler, Signor Tyler." As soon as the tourists were past, the frantic hand signals erupted again, as did our laughter. Deciding to go into the hotel, I strode through the high-ceilinged foyer, past reception and through the tall French doors. The table was free, where we had sat every day of our time in Sanvicci, where the terrazzo sea-facing balustrade met the stucco wall of the hotel. I sat down and ordered a beer from a white-jacketed waiter. Feeling the sea breeze cool my face, I looked into the cerulean ocean and tried to picture Therese lapping in the waves, but memory let me down. Instead, I stared, buoyed on the endless roll of sea.

Having had a late lunch, I wasn't in the mood for dinner. Still a little unsettled after last night, I resisted the urge to stop at the little supermarket to buy wine. I smiled when the manager wished me, "Buona sera," as I passed him on the way back to my hotel room. Once inside, I ran a tepid bath and lay in it till the water chilled, letting the sweat of the short day soak off and my skin cool to a comfortable temperature. I stretched out on the bed. In four short years, everything had changed.

I had been dining with Therese in a little trattoria on the beachfront, trying not to order something stereotypically Italian, laughing at her ordering spaghetti for the third night in a row. We joked about making a honeymoon baby and silently hoped each night that we had. It would be almost three years later before she would thrust a urine-drenched stick into my hand and cry "Finally" into my shoulder. A month later, she would be gone.

We had arrived late at the theatre in a taxi. Therese exited on the traffic side of the car. The driver hadn't yet pulled up his handbrake. The car slid back only an inch or so, but shielding her tummy, she jumped back into the road. I don't know if she ever saw the other car. Everything changed in an instant. No one tells you how to be a widower at thirty-four years old. I had never considered losing Therese at any age.

I reached over and opened the bedside drawer, lifting out the box of pills. I had been saving my Diazepam prescription for the last four months. One hundred and twelve pills. I had taken one last night. According to the internet, one hundred and eleven pills would not be enough. What would work is two bottles of prosecco to wash the pills down as I stride down the beach towards the setting sun, sinking with it into the sea. I had planned one more night, but a year had already been too long. Since booking this trip, my numbness had slowly thawed, and the pulse, which sometimes threatened to split my chest in two, had calmed. This trip was going home to Therese. I checked my watch; still enough time to go back to the little supermarket and buy the wine that would help take me to her. I sat up on the bed and quickly dressed in today's clothes. As I bent to tie my shoes, I saw below, through the glass doors, a little boy of maybe two years old, tan-skinned and black-haired. He ran in circles around the statue of Santa Fina, waving his hands as if chasing something. His head rolled back in laughter; too big for his body, it looked as if it might fall off in glee. I opened the doors. Just beyond his reach, a dove flapped, dropping to almost within his reach and swooping off again, never more than a metre away or so from him.

In the piazza, beautiful people paraded, couples ate dinner and drank wine, but no one seemed to notice the little boy. Turning back to him, he had moved beyond the statue, following the dove, towards the steps of the church. His giggles seemed to bubble up and into my room. The bird glided further away from the little boy, who tottered in its direction, closer to the steps. Still, no adult looked his way. Like a feather in the wind, the dove swept up and landed halfway up the steep stone steps. The boy's head bobbed with laughter as he ran to the first step and clasped it with both hands, pausing to look up at the dove. My heart thudded in my chest. I shouted, "Hey, ragazzi!" but no one looked my way. I cursed how useless my few Italian nouns were, with no knowledge of the verbs to make sense of them.

The dove floated down to the boy, just two steps away from him. He squealed, reached out both hands for the bird, and clasped them together, grasping air as the dove took flight again. As he raised his head to see the bird land at the top of the steps, he toppled slightly before righting himself with a giggle and reaching for the next stone step. He pulled his little bare knees from one step to the next. Still, no one looked. The thudding filled my throat, and a trickle of sweat dripped from under my arm. "Ragazzo!" The boy turned and smiled at me, blue eyes striking in his dark face. He clambered up the next step. "Stop!" But he ignored me this time. Why could no one hear me screaming, "Ragazzi"? When the little boy reached seven or eight steps, I hurdled over furniture, through doors, down staircases, through more doors. Arriving at the statue and running towards the church steps, I could not see the boy.

I swung round to look at the diners and strollers, searching between arms and legs for the little black head. "Il ragazzo?" I shouted, but no one replied. Some muttered, and some turned their gaze back to their plates. "Il ragazzo?" I repeated louder still, but they all stared emphatically away from me. I walked around in circles, tracing the boy's tracks, but there was no sign that he had ever been there. I climbed the steps as if he might be hiding on the higher steps out of my line of vision. I reached the top step and tried the door of the church, still locked. I twisted my neck to look at the open doorway on my balcony as if he might be there. As I started down the steps, I was stopped by a noise behind me. The cooing of a dove from the window ledge of the church, looking directly at me. It swept onto my balcony.

Acutely aware of how I appeared to onlookers, I forced myself to steady my walk back to my room. Just like the woman in red the previous night, I was sure the dove would have vanished but on opening the door, I heard the gentle flap of wings. The bird was perched on the bedside table, its eyes following me as I walked into the room and closed the door. I inched around the bed towards it, its head twisted to keep me in sight. When I was nearly within reaching distance, the dove rose into the air, flew around me and out through the open balcony doors. On the floor, in front of the bedside table, lay the box of pills and two white feathers.

I lifted the box of pills, put it back in the drawer and lay down on the bed, the feathers cradled in my left hand. Gazing through the open door at the roof of the church of Santa Fina against the blue-black sky, I fell into a dreamless sleep.

My final morning in Sanvicci, I awoke still fully dressed and in the same position as I had fallen asleep. I raised my hands to rub my face and remembered the feathers in my hand. They were gone. Instead in my hand, curled a long strand of hair, auburn, almost maroon. As my eyes filled, a shiver rolled from my head to my toes. Therese was calling me home to her.

I packed my case, leaving one change of clothes in the wardrobe and some toiletries in the bathroom and went downstairs for breakfast. Sitting at a rickety table looking up at La Cappella di Santa Fina, I ordered un caffè. The day was bright and warm. I felt my body weight against the iron chair, felt the cobbles through my shoes on my feet. My breath in time with my heart, I listened to the noise of the birds and early traffic, picked out friendly cries of "prego," "buongiorno' and "ciao." Another noise began to mingle in my reverie, a low moaning. Sobs punctuated by mangled Italian pleas. Behind the statue of Santa Fina, a crooked-backed old man waved his arms and shouted at the church and passers-by, who ignored all of him. Still shouting, he began to climb the steps when a burst of laughter erupted. He swivelled and fell from his step onto his face. I jumped up to help him. I took his arm and helped him lift himself into a seated position. He smelt of stale sweat and staler beer. He looked into my eyes, whispered, "Grazie," got on his feet and stumbled off, looking once over his shoulder.

Sitting down again, I signalled for my bill. The waiter brought il conto unusually promptly. He looked at me and said,

"You are a good man."

"Why did no one else help him?"

"He is old and, um, well-known? Often, he comes here. Always shouting."

"Oh? Why is that?"

"He is angry."

"With the hotel? With people?"

"No, with the cappella."

"The cappella?"

"The chapel, the church, yes, but more with the monache, with the nuns. He blames them for taking his daughter."

"His daughter is in a convent?"

"Many years ago, it was not good for a woman who was not married to have a baby. But his daughter had a baby. At that time, most families would send away the girl, but Pietro said no. He said Jesus's own mother was not married. He kept the girl and her child in his house. But every Sunday, the madre superiora would visit him and tell him that it was not right and that the child must go to a good family who has no children."

"To be adopted?"

"After some time, the young woman became sick for a long time. She was dying. The priest refused to give her the last rites because she did not repent of her sin. At last, Pietro gave the child to the nun's orphans' home, and the priest gave Pietro's daughter the last rites."

"Pietro lost his child and his grandchild?"

"The day after his daughter received the last rites, she started to heal. It was a miracle! In one week, she was able to walk again. She asked for her child, but Pietro said he was with friends. Finally, he told her the truth. Gloria was angry and went to the orphans' home, but they would not let her see her son."

"How awful."

"She went back there every day and was told to go away. One night, she broke into the orphans' home through the cappella. She searched the whole building, but her child was not there. She made much noise, and the madre superiora came and told her to go away. Her son was living with his new family, a good Christian family."

"She must have been heartbroken?"

"Of course, but worse was to come. The nun was not telling the truth. Gloria left the orphans' home and sat on the steps of the cappella for a long time, heartbroken and sobbing. A young nun, a novice? She came to her to tell her that her son had not left the home at all but was buried there. Not long after arriving there, he had fallen down some steps, and he broke his neck."

"No."

"Yes, and Gloria was crazed with anger and grief. She banged at the doors, but they were locked against her. She searched for a way to get into the building but could find no door unlocked. She climbed the high wall to the garden but she fell off the top of the wall into the garden. The young novice called after her, but there was no answer. Afraid of what the madre superiora would do to her, the young nun ran to get the local police. Gloria's body was found beside a small patch of freshly dug earth, where her son was buried. The police started an investigation and found bodies of other little children."

"What had happened to the other children?"

"I do not know, but the orphans' home was closed, and the nuns all moved away."

"What happened to the novice nun?"

"The young nun, she left the convent. Maybe the madre superiora threw her out. The girl was an orphan herself and had grown up in the home. When she left, having no other skills for the outside world, there were rumours that she had to enter a very different profession. After some years, she returned to Sanvicci, La Capella, in the middle of the night. She hung herself on the altar."

An icy chill gripped my neck and tightened its way down my back. I paid the waiter and returned to my room. Sitting on the bed, I looked out at the casino and the chapel to my right and at the sea behind the old buildings to my left. As I stared into the blue nothingness, the woman outside the cappella came into my mind's eye. The young boy, on the steps, looking into my eyes. I lifted myself off the bed and walked downstairs, through the lobby and out the hotel doors. I glanced at La Cappella di Santa Fina as I pushed past the iron chairs and tables.

Walking away from the church, I searched for another way into the cappella or the orphanage. The hotel was built flush with an expensive, glass-fronted boutique, but beside the boutique was a narrow alley. The buildings on either side of the alley were four or five storeys high, creating a dark tunnel. The only light was a trapezium of sunshine at its entrance. Stepping into the alley, the heat and noise of the day stopped dead. A breeze blew under my shirt as I moved further into the passage. I turned to look back, already detached from the life beyond, as I slipped away from the light.

In here, the walls were rough, grey and unpainted. Although I could see swaths of blue above the walls, little light seemed to reach me. A screech tore at my ears as a black cat bolted past me towards the bright street at the end of the alley. I turned the corner and stopped. Facing a high stone wall, a black figure sobbed and scratched at the wall. I was fixed to the spot. I had to see it. I inched closer. The high-pitched sobbing became louder. Closing in on the figure, I recognised the black garb of a nun. I reached a hand for her shoulder. She screamed and swivelled her face towards me. The blue hue of the dead faced me. I leapt backwards. As I did, the nun seemed to melt into the wall. In her place appeared a sturdy wooden gate. Swallowing back the metallic taste in my mouth, I edged towards the gate. I put my ear to it but could hear nothing on the other side. Slowly, the gate swung open. My face flooded with bright sunlight, and my ears filled with the sound of children's laughter.

Light exploded as I opened the gate to the courtyard. Little children ran in circles, chasing doves and laughing. Two dark-haired women played amongst them, sweeping up and tickling some of the younger children. Under a tree dripping with orange blossoms sat a woman with a baby to her chest, her right hand caressing the child's auburn, almost maroon, hair. As she lifted her head, I called out Therese's name.

She did not respond. I called again but she moved further from me. As I began to walk towards her, she moved towards the women amongst the children. The children flocked to her, climbing over each other to coo the baby. I called again. One of the women took the baby, and Therese knelt in a circle with the children, singing something in Italian, a nursery rhyme, with them.

Seeing the smiling children's faces engrossed in Therese's gentle attention, my eyes stung as I realised that I should not call after her again. I turned to leave the sunny courtyard. Looking back, the women and children gathered and smiled at me. The light from the courtyard of the orphanage illuminated my way. The alley was no longer dark but lit in a warm, golden glow. My body was overcome with a warmth and safety I had not felt since being wrapped in my mother's arms as a boy.

I returned to my hotel room, opened the balcony doors and looked at the Statue of Santa Fina as I emptied the bedside drawer. I walked to the little bathroom and pushed each of the pills out of the blister pack and into the toilet.

I checked out of the hotel quickly and declined their offer to phone me a taxicab. Across the cobbles, I wheeled my case out of the doors and headed in the direction of the train station. Inside the doors of Sanvicci train station, I successfully bought a single ticket from a cantankerous machine and descended the steps to the underground platform. I did not have to wait long for the train. Alone, I sat in a compartment dully lit by flickering fluorescent tubes. The train jolted as we started into the dark tunnel. The compartment fell black as the tube bulb dimmed. We travelled along in darkness until the train finally escaped into the light of the evening sunset. Through the window, on the sapphire sea, danced ribbons of purple and orange as the sun melted into the horizon. I breathed in, leaned my head back on the seat and slept.

TALL DARK STRANGER

*P*olice *are investigating a serious sexual assault on a woman near Belvoir Zoo in North Belfast. The thirty-two-year-old was attacked on the Antrim Road shortly after 8pm on Wednesday, twenty fourth of October. Detectives have appealed for any witnesses who may have seen the attack or anyone acting suspiciously in the area to come forward. Police have said the attacker may have hidden in the shadows of a house on Antrim Road, then followed the victim before dragging her into a nearby wood and attacking her. According to detectives, this is the fourth such attack in the area in as many weeks. Police are appealing for anyone with any information to come forward and assist their investigation.*

Sarah knew that at least one other woman had been attacked but had not reported it to police. There were likely more. She had tried jogged earlier in the evening these last two weeks, but darkness was steadily eating the bright evenings. Soon, she would be left with the dilemma of either not jogging or jogging alone in the dark.

Not jogging until this beast was caught would be the sensible option, but Sarah needed to run. For a long time, as darkness descended, so did Sarah's mood. The long, dank winter ground her spirit. Just two years ago, it seemed that the blackness was about to overtake her, and she took the road that runs only one way. Sarah's mother, in an uncharacteristic display of good timing, had discovered her and rung an ambulance.

After a short stay in hospital while she recovered from her physical injuries, Sarah was prescribed pills and diagnosed with severe Seasonal Affective Disorder. Being SAD each winter seemed a little self-indulgent and not a little pathetic, like she was merely pining for the sun. Doesn't everyone do that? Most people are not desperate enough to try to end their lives because the days are getting shorter. The pills did not help much, nor did the "talking therapy."

One morning last year, Sarah had slept in for work; the pills made her a little groggy in the mornings, so this was not an uncommon occurrence. Linda, her supervisor, had asked to speak to her the previous day. Linda tilted her head a lot and made sympathetic noises behind pressed lips but managed to fit the words "final warning" into her little staff welfare meeting. As Sarah approached the bus stop, she saw the bus pull away. She would have to run to catch it. She grabbed tight onto her bag and, after faltering a little, sprinted to the bus. The bus gained speed, and Sarah did too. She became level with the entrance door, banged on it, ran, waved at the driver, and ran again to keep up. The driver slowed, and Sarah leapt onto the bus. As she paid her fare and thanked the driver, a strange twitch afflicted her face – she was smiling, out of breath and actually laughing as she sat down.

Almost missing the bus, Sarah made a discovery – running could save her life. From that day, Sarah ran for her life. Most days, she jogged. On days when she was weighed down, she ran off her burdens. Soon, Sarah no longer needed happy pills. She weaned herself off the counselling sessions, too. All she needed to be happy was to run. Not running was not an option.

Sarah trotted out of her house on the Antrim Road, the sky a bruised beige. She stopped to stretch her calves and thighs, loosening up her lower back before continuing on her route. She was almost level with cars on their way home from work, soon surpassing them as the colour drained from the sky. Streetlights blinked on as she jogged, sprinted, then jogged again through the carpet of yellow leaves lining the road. Her breathing fast and steady, matched the rhythmic thud of her steps. Reaching the bottom of the steep sweep towards the zoo gates, Sarah saw the last of the daylight surrender to the night. She always ran up this hill. The view at the top over the lit-up city and Belfast Lough made the painful legs worthwhile. This was her midway point. Sarah stopped at the pinnacle, her breath and pulse slowing towards normality as her eyes picked out various buildings and none in the array of streetlights beyond the trees.

The chill of sweat on her skin broke Sarah from her trance, and she began to walk down the hill. To her left, half-nude trees trembled in the breeze. The traffic had eased. The air was still. At the bottom, Sarah would retrace her steps, cantering her way back. A hundred metres from home, Sarah's skin tightened across her upper back. She turned her head quickly but could see no one behind her. Her stomach lurched at a sudden rustle beside her ear. She made to sprint but screamed at the shape flashing before her eyes. She stumbled off the pavement, one foot on the road, as a car screeched and blew its horn. Jumping back onto the pavement, Sarah saw the beast. A squirrel. She laughed out loud and wiped sweat from her neck, looking around to see if anyone had seen her. No one, but she could have sworn the squirrel thumbed its nose before bouncing up a tree with a pinecone in its mouth. After deeply inhaling, Sarah sprinted home.

The next day at work, Sarah could do no right. Linda stomped about the office and handed work back to Sarah like a dissatisfied teacher, telling her she must do better, "And Sarah, we need to talk about your flexi-time." Sarah waited until Linda had left the office for the day before logging off and making her way to the bus stop. It had been a postcard autumn day, all blue skies, wisps of cloud, leaves sprinkling gold and rust in the breeze, but darkness was clawing at the day.

By the time Sarah was home and back on the street for her run, the only light in the sky was from a fattening moon. The air cooled the breath in her lungs, but still, the day's struggles knotted in her throat. She needed to run it off quickly; skipping her stretching, she hit the ground sprinting. Home-time traffic had long since subsided, and few cars passed her as Sarah coursed through the fallen foliage. Each stride lifted her farther from the petty annoyances of the day. Nearing the ascent to the zoo, Sarah's pace picked up. She attacked the hill, greedy for the pacifying view atop. Reaching the hillside gates of the zoo, Sarah crouched down and hugged her legs to her chest. Her shins burned. She pointed her toes, stretched her legs, and tried to shake the pain away to no avail. Finally, she decided to wait out the pain. She closed her eyes, stretching her head back as if drinking in the moonlight. The moon floated on the lough, mesmerising Sarah like a hypnotist's pendulum.

With her mind clear and her breathing balanced, Sarah made her way downhill. Her shins still ached and burned; she would have to walk home but the beauty of the evening had erased all urgency in any case. She made her way along the road, breathing deeply and slowly, keeping a vigil on the rising moon, and examining silhouetted trees whose leaves had all but abandoned them. A creak amongst the trees brought her attention to the fact that she was at the exact spot the mischievous squirrel had pranked her last night. Behind her, a branch twisted in the still night. She flicked her head around. A scratching noise in the trees. She moved closer to the trees and made a clicking noise, trying to entice the squirrel into view. All quiet, all still, she stood stock still, squinting through boughs and golden leaves, trying to make out the creature. Finally, the cold air pressed her to start walking again. She sauntered home, careful not to stress her sore shins and wondering if squirrels ever slept.

Police have apprehended a suspect in a series of serious sexual assaults on women in the Antrim Road area of north Belfast. The arrest comes days after the latest attack. It is believed detectives have arrested the thirty-nine-year-old man after an undercover operation last night. The suspect was

*arrested when he attempted to pull a policewoman into a thicket on the
Antrim Road.*

*Detectives have appealed for a woman seen on security camera footage
from Belvoir Zoo around 8pm last night to contact them.*

Sarah's heart pulsed in her neck as she read that last sentence.
She phoned the police number printed underneath the article.

Back home after her visit to the police station, the cup of tea
in Sarah's hand felt too heavy. It shook as she brought it to her
lips. After confirming that she was the woman in the video,
police explained to Sarah that the attacker had jumped out of a
copse and attempted to pull an undercover police officer into the
trees. The detective showed her the body cam footage of the
attack. Sarah's breath caught as she recognised the spot where
she had looked for the squirrel. The detective explained that
Sarah had passed the spot minutes before the attacker tried to
capture the policewoman. Police had told Sarah that the attacker
was likely already waiting in the trees when she had passed. She
wondered why the attacker had not chosen her. The detective
agreed that it was strange and on questioning the suspect about
this, he explained that Sarah was walking with a man. Police had
checked the video again, but Sarah was alone. The attacker,
however, insisted that beside Sarah had walked a tall, dark man.

PÚCA

Ú na scrunched her shoulders towards her ears, dropped her short knife into the sink and stretched her neck to the left, then to the right. She looked through the small square of a window at her kitchen sink onto the field behind her house. Rusty, mustard smudges clung to the dark limbs of trees stretching into the tea-stained sky. The smoke of next door's unswept chimney seeped through the cracks around the window, mingling with the sweet tang of the raw turnip in her left hand. Most people carved pumpkins these days, but Úna preferred the old ways. As the torturous notes of *The Kerry Polka* ripped through the house from her son Michael's fiddle practice in the living room, Úna raised an eyebrow in silent prayer for patience.

"Michael, would you give me a hand with these turnips?"

"In a minute."

Úna inhaled deeply and slowly exhaled as the final notes of the score assaulted her eardrums.

"Awk Ma, why don't you just use pumpkins, like everyone else?"

"Your daddy always carved turnips, and so shall I." A moment's silence hung between them.

"What are you dressing up as this year, Michael?"

"Ah, I'm too old for that carry-on, Ma."

"You are not! Sure, don't I dress up as a witch every year?"

"Dead scary," Michael rolled his eyes.

"Don't blame me when the faeries run away with you so," his mother teased.

"Ma, it's just not the same anymore. Without him."

Úna turned back to the sink, digging at the inside of the turnip with a spoon, "I know, son."

She had learnt at school and from her father that this was the time of the year when the veil between the worlds of the living and the dead slipped away, allowing the dead to walk among the living again. Úna wondered if, like her, Michael had quietly longed these last two Halloweens for his father to pay them even a fleeting visit or to send an unmistakable sign and if he, too, had been disappointed.

Halloween arrived as slips of blue swished through the creamy sky. Naked treetops, T.V. aerials, blackbirds and escaped litter danced jigs in the sky, keeping time, each in their own orbits. Úna thought back to when she was a girl; of homemade costumes and hard plastic masks called false faces; of kitchen tables heavy with nuts, coconuts, apple tarts, barmbrack, toffee apples; of children carrying lanterns carved from turnips, lit with stumps of candle behind hideously pared eyes; of parties with children playing games with apples on string, snap apple, she thought it was called, or duck-apple where they half-drowned themselves trying to bite into the fruit bobbing in a bowl of water, gnashing at the elusive globe stabbed with a coin; of fireworks, most of which fizzled out before they reached the starry sky; and of the scary stories her father told her, of how the lanterns and costumes scared off the evil entities which were freed to walk on earth for that night only. She never left a door or window open in the house after dark on Halloween for fear an evil spirit would enter, and she always, particularly in the last two years, left baked gifts to welcome departed loved ones.

"Michael, come on down and show me your costume," shouted Úna up the stairs.

Michael came downstairs in a red tracksuit, "Ma, will you stop with that nonsense! I'm not dressing up or doing any of that kids' stuff!"

Michael ducked under Úna's arm, which was stretched onto the wooden newel post at the bottom of the stairs and ran out the front door, slamming it hard.

Dusk swept the light from the sky, and windows lit up with glowing orange, purple and green fairy lights. The littlest children began to appear on the lane, one hand carrying felt cauldrons to collect sweets and treats, the other held tightly by indulgent parents. Úna checked her watch as she distributed chocolate coins amongst the latest clutch of children gathered at her door. Michael had still not come home, and it would be dark soon. She was always uneasy in these weeks when the seasons shifted from light to dark, looking over her shoulder in the garden scooping coal for the fire, catching wisps of shadows in the reflections in the windowpane as she drew the curtains, shuddering in the doorway as she came home to an unlit house. As she was closing her door, she saw Mrs Martin shuffling down the lane with her wheeled shopping bag behind her. She hurried down the short path, took the shopping from the old lady, and walked with her to her own house. Shutting Mrs Martin's door behind her, she noticed she had not closed her own front door. As she rushed back home and through her garden gate, she was pushed aside. A dark hooded shape ran into her house before her.

"Stop!" she shouted.

"It's only me, Ma," he shouted back, bounding up the stairs.

Michael? She rushed in and was about to follow him up the stairs when at her door began another shaky chorus of "Halloween is coming on..." Ignoring the latest group of door-to-door children to check on Michael, she was stopped by the same tune from Michael's fiddle echoing from his room. Although not a complicated tune, he was playing it perfectly. The air haunted the stairwell and wafted over the children's heads out into the dark night. The children had stopped singing and held their bags and baskets out for their treats, which Úna passed out with refrains of "Happy Halloween," which she hated for its modernity. She shut the door and headed upstairs again. From Michael's room floated a perfect air of one of her favourite tunes, *The Dawning of the Day*. She had never heard Michael play so well before and felt bad for her lack of patience at times with his playing. She wanted to knock on his door to ask if he was ok, but she was utterly mesmerised by the music, and as another song began, she instead sat on the landing, eyes closed, drinking in his beautiful tunes.

The next morning, finding Michael's bedroom empty and his bed unslept in, Úna rushed downstairs and into the little dining room which led to the kitchen. Atop the dining table sat Michael, surrounded by crumbly chunks of apple tart, shells tumbling from the nut bowls onto the swirly patterned carpet, orange peel dripping from the ceiling lampshade, multi-coloured foil sweet wrappers everywhere. Beside Michael lay a claw hammer, his head tilted back, sucking milk from the jagged edge of the smashed coconut.

"Michael..."

When he lowered his head, she saw a plastic face mask sitting on the crown of his head and her own witch's cape tied at his neck. He grinned at her, leapt from the table and threw his arms around her.

"My sweet Úna," he said.

"Michael, what's wrong with you?" she asked, pushing him back to look him in the eyes.

"Michael?" the boy said, "Sorry, Mam."

Úna's hand flew to her chest and rested there; she stood speechless as the boy slipped out of the room and bounded upstairs. It wasn't possible, she told herself. That's not... The most gorgeous tune weaved through the air. What was that tune? She thought she knew it from somewhere and yet not at all. It felt to her as if the music was taking up the broken threads of her soul and embroidering them into something whole again. She sat on the old sofa and wept great shuddering tears, hugging herself tightly until no more tears would fall; still, he played and played.

Over the next months, Michael was quiet except when playing his fiddle. Any chore she asked of him, he obliged without protest. He sat with Úna anytime she asked, although he did not speak unless spoken to. Every day, Úna asked for a different tune and every day, Michael played the requested tune without hesitation or fault. When the Christmas break was finished, and Michael went back to school, Úna went to his room to gather the inevitable piles of forgotten dishes, cups, stained sports gear, dirty jeans and odd socks. Instead, she found a room with not a thing out of place; the bed made with tight crisp hospital corners, pillows arranged just so, books lining the shelves, spines all facing outwards, ordered according to size.

On the shining mahogany desk, in its velvet-lined case, reposed the fiddle which had lit up her soul these recent days and nights. She looked about for the sheet music with which Michael must have been practising but could find it nowhere; the only music she could find was a beginners' book of basic traditional Irish tunes, but nothing that held the notes to the spellbinding tunes Michael had been playing for her. Strange, maybe he had the music in his school bag, although why take the sheet music but leave the instrument at home?

Michael blew in through the door with the cold, earthy scent of winter on his clothes, his cheeks ruddy, and his leather school shoes covered in clods of mud and grass. Úna looked at her watch, "Michael, where have you been? Why aren't you in school; it's only half past one?" He stared through her, then thundered past her, straight to his room, slamming the door, but before she had even set foot on the first stair, Michael unleashed an uproarious jig which tumbled down the stairs, bounced through the hall, flapped and slapped around the kitchen, knocking crockery off the pine sideboard, throwing cutlery in the air, opening and closing cupboard doors like washing blowing in the wind.

The whole house thrummed with the terrible energy of the tune. The front door shook and rattled in its frame. Úna took the handle to try and hold it still. She pulled and pulled with every fibre of her strength. The door flung open, and Úna landed on the floor at the bottom of the staircase. Black silk ribbons danced through the doorway, swirling, floating and coming together on the globe atop the newel post. Úna must have banged her head, for looking down on her was a huge black crow. Úna had always been terrified of crows, haunted by images forged by her father of lambs with their eyes pecked out by the cruel avians, but this bird with its satin night-sky plumes quivering, its strong neck and deep glistening opal eyes, quieted Úna's beating heart.

Enthralled by its black diamond eye, she saw reflected there her own image lying at the bottom of the stairs. Like an invisible silken thread entwining them, Úna's eye was fixed on the crow's eye. Her miniature image began to move in reverse. Here she fell, there was Michael running on the stairs, then at the door. The crow began to hum, a sound nothing like the normal caw-caw you would expect, but a tune as if from an oboe, a hymn from childhood that she could not quite remember the words to. Úna felt as if she were falling deep into a heavy sleep, but her eyes were wide open, watching the crow's eye as it told her its story. Úna felt wrapped in the kindest arms, taken under a strong, warm wing.

She saw herself in those first weeks of winter after Halloween, at peace with Michael's music. She looked in at herself from outside the kitchen window, seeing her eyes raised in frustration at the tuneless hawking he produced. When had he become so talented, how had it happened almost overnight?

Úna, now perched in the half-bare, blazing cherry tree in her front garden, saw Michael run out the door on Halloween, for the first time seeing the teary rivulets darkening the downy hair on his upper lip. Looking onto the street beyond the path to her house, Úna saw other things which she had not seen that Halloween night. Walking alongside Mrs Martin was her crooked-backed husband, his hand on her elbow taking some of her weight; Mr Martin who had died ten years past. Skipping in the road, lollipop in her mouth was little Lily McGahon, who had slipped into the river beyond the woods on her seventh birthday while Úna herself was just a girl living in the same house she did now. A black and tan mongrel ran to the base of the tree and started barking up at her.

When she looked down, the dog stopped, and she recognised Bran, who grew up with her and left her on her sixteenth birthday. An idea, a hope, came to Úna, and she looked up and down the street for Michael's dad, Francie. Could he be... A wheezing, whistling guffaw, and muffled screams pulled her eye towards the forest. The awful laughter came from a creature the likes of which she had never seen. At first, she thought it was a dog, robbed of its fur, such was the shape of its legs, but no; the head was like a gargoyle from the chapel roof, misshapen with one too many eyes and a slick, grey, forked tongue whipping and slipping from its open mouth of a hundred sharp, yellow teeth, spittle dripping from each of the fangs. Its arms were long, a monkey's, with its humanoid hands, one of which held the rope tethering a pair of hands, the other gripping the neck of a young boy. It took her too long to realise the boy was Michael. Úna tried to jump from the tree, but when she looked down, she was no longer in the tree but back in the hallway of her house, watching her front door as the hooded figure rushed in. Time stopped, and she looked into the face within that hood. Of course, the face did not belong to Michael. Still, it was familiar.

It was a face she had not seen in a very long time and one she had never seen in its youth, but slowly, she recognised her own uncle. The figure, her uncle, bounded up the stairs, and the music began, just as it had that Halloween night.

Úna remembered the last time she saw Louis, his eye already bruising red, and his lip busted all over his face, her father rubbing his grazed fist, still clenched. She remembered her confusion at her father's words to him, "Get out and don't come back. Over my dead body, you'll be near another child in this house." Úna's older brother stopped having nightmares when he left. She closed her eyes, and when she opened them again, she was back lying at the foot of the stairs, the crow gone, the music stopped. Of course, she must have been concussed, but the dream had felt so real, and she had a new sense of something, an awakening, a knowing. She looked up the stairs, and Michael stood at the top, smiling down at her with that familiar grin which was not his own. Louis. Vision, or concussion, Úna knew now. A púca had taken her son and allowed this evil being to take his place. She had to get Michael back, but a familiar feeling crept over her skin looking at the face on top of the stairs, a feeling she had not felt in thirty years, something as close to evil as she had ever known. She recalled the many ways she had slipped from his grip, ducking from his hand petting her head, scooping up Bran when he made to lift her, calling for her mother when she found herself alone with him. She did not know then what she was trying to escape from, just that she must escape. Now she knew that she must get him out of her house and get her son back. She realised that all this time, she had allowed herself to be blinded by his music. It was the same trick he had used when she was young; Louis was a prodigious musician, which earned him respect and admiration throughout the village. He had blinded almost everyone with his music. This must be the last tune he played.

Úna spent days, nights, weeks, and months trying desperately to work out how to get rid of the imposter and to get back her son. Although she believed in the old ways, did she really believe that a púca had sneaked into her home and snatched her son? She knew of the old stories of changelings, but it was always young children who were stolen in those tales. It seemed unthinkable. Yet Michael, if it was Michael, had changed. He was quiet and rarely left his room. He played his fiddle from when he woke until after Úna went to sleep. She had found him one night at 3am playing a slow, slumbery tune in the kitchen. When she asked him what he was doing, he stopped playing and walked past her without a word.

Sometimes, she looked up from peeling potatoes or lighting the fire to see him staring at her with her uncle's grin on his face and her blood chilled in her veins. At times, she felt like she was playing an unspoken game with him: finding a misplaced kitchen knife under her chair cushion, opening the dining room door to a gust of cooking gas from an unlit oven, catching sight of copper on the gnawed through power cable just as she was about to switch on the television. Úna began to fear her son or rather the shape of a thing that was in her son's place.

One morning, bleary-eyed, Úna tripped at the top of the stairs but, with one hand, had caught hold of the bannister, her other hand grasping a violin string pulled taut across the stairs. She stormed into Michael's room.

"What is wrong with you? Why would you do that?" she screamed in his impassive face. He continued playing, staring into her eyes. She snatched the fiddle from him and slammed the bedroom door shut behind her. In her own bedroom, she pulled out a hold-all wedged behind her wardrobe, pushing the fiddle into the space and tucked the carry-all back in place, hiding the fiddle. Michael stayed in his room for the rest of the day, and the house was silent. Úna felt herself able to breathe for the first time since Halloween. She had not realised how intrusive such beautiful music could be to her sanity. How could she have thought such mad ideas, thought that Michael was some sort of changeling? That her son's body was possessed by a malignant ancestor? She realised that she and Michael were clearly suffering some delayed effects of grief. Maybe she had gone a little crazy herself. Michael did not come down from his room at dinner time and she decided to check on him. There was no answer when she knocked on his door, so she opened it and entered quietly. In his bed, Michael's chest rose and fell slowly, in rhythm with the breaths that whistled softly from his nose. His eyes closed in a deep sleep. Úna went downstairs and read in the firelight until she started to drift into slumber. In bed, she fell asleep quicker than she had in months, her rest sumptuously endless and dreamless. Her breath was knocked from her chest. A great weight stopped her air. Her eyes opened onto the dark and saw Michael sitting atop her chest, knees pinning her arms to her sides. The fiddle under his chin, the bow in his hand like a knife, hacking a demonic tune as he bounced in time, jiggling his body closer and closer to Úna's neck. A billion stars blinked in her eyes, but from somewhere, she was filled with a force that lifted Michael off her chest and slammed him against the bedroom wall. Breathless, she screamed at him to get out as he rubbed the back of his head, giggling. He ran from the room and slammed his bedroom door. His maniacal laughter was soon replaced with the gnawing notes of the fiddle, which did not cease all night.

Úna had to save her son and herself.

The fiddle held some sort of power; was Michael playing the fiddle, or was Michael the instrument? The fiddle had to go.

Weeks passed. Michael rarely spoke to Úna. He did not eat the meals she prepared. When she caught rare glimpses of him, he seemed deathly thin and pale. Time was running out. Spring and summer had come and gone, and an autumn chill outdoors drew score with the imperishable cold in her house. In early October, as the nights began consuming the edges of the day and the green of the woods that cradled her house dulled into shades of yellow and brown, Úna coaxed Michael into her living room as she switched on lamps and lit the fire. He held the fiddle in his hand, as always.

"Michael, would you play my favourite tune?" Úna asked. He thought for a while, then began playing. When he was finished, she said to him, throwing another log onto the fire, "That was a fine tune and so well played. It's not the one I was thinking of, though. Would you play another for me?" He closed his eyes for a moment, then drew his bow over the strings again. The flames from the fire danced on the rough, old, white-washed walls of her living room. The notes of the tune seemed to carry her off somewhere familiar, warm, and safe; she raised her eyebrows, trying to prise open her heavy eyelids. As her head began to nod, she inhaled deep and hard, "Not that one. Play the tune you played for me when I was just a little girl."

He snapped open his eyes and stared at her, tongues of fire reflected in his pupils as she took her chance, snatched the fiddle from him and threw it straight onto the lapping, snapping, licking flames. His scream rattled the windows. Úna threw herself on top of him as he reached for the fire. He flailed below her and scratched at her arms and shoulders, trying to dislodge her, but the body below her was still a child's body, no matter what possessed it, and she managed to hold onto him until the fiddle was too consumed by the fire to be saved. When his screams fell into tears, she released him. "Michael?" she asked, "Is it you?" He looked up at her from beneath thick, damp lashes, not meeting her own eye, shame-faced.

"It's ok, son," she said. His lips drew into a small tight smile, still not looking at her, his lips widened into a grin, his face seemed to split at the mouth as his smile consumed his face, his eyes puckered on the horrible mask. The jagged-toothed, too-wide smile filled his head, filling his body. Úna felt her legs weaken and fell to the sofa as he seemed to double in size and cower over her like a feral cat ready to rip apart its tiny prey. Then he was gone. His bedroom door slammed, the whole house mimicking its clatter, then nothing but the beating of Úna's heart and the crackle of the fire. Úna's tears were loud and ferocious.

Úna's house was silent for a week; no music and no sign of Michael. He may have been in his room, but she neither dared nor cared to check. He was not her son. She wanted Michael back but had no idea what to do. There was no one to help. She felt more alone than she had since her husband had died. She had lost them both. She no longer wanted to live. She spent her days in bed, occasionally eating something from the larder that could be heated and consumed without any thought. She felt herself fading away, and she had no desire to fight it. One night, she dreamed of Michael and his father, Francie. Michael was just a baby, and his father held both his hands as he practised walking. Gradually, Francie let go of his son's hands and the boy tottered along a few steps, giggling at his achievement before realising his father no longer held his hands and falling on his bottom. Francie scooped him up and told Michael, "Don't worry, I'll never let you go."

Úna woke, washed, dressed, and went into the kitchen to make breakfast. She looked at the calendar, just days till Halloween. She rubbed her arms and cold crept out of the old stone walls. She hadn't lit a fire in weeks and a chill gripped the house as she scooped out the cinders and brushed up the pale ashes, the sound of a fiddle cut through the air like a broken bottle on skin. She opened the kitchen door; the music came from upstairs in Michael's room. Where did he get another fiddle? And how? Would he never stop tormenting her? Úna snatched her coat from where it hung on a peg on the coat rail that Francie had made for her at the bottom of the stairs. She ran through the door and onto her lane. She did not know where she was going, but she had to leave. She had to walk away. She could not stay in that house. At the end of her path, Mrs Martin stood, scarf pulled tight around her shoulders, head bent, talking to another of their neighbours, "Úna, did you hear about..." but Úna had neither the time nor patience for small talk or gossip, and she rushed past the women with her eyes fixed firmly ahead. Úna marched towards the woods, her breath white plumes before her. It was too cold for this time of year, winter overtaking autumn. Her feet crushed the leaves of ginger and burgundy that speckled the grass until the leeched green gave way to brown earth leading into the forest. When they were teenagers, Úna and Francie would sneak into the forest away from their friends. Despite the bawdy rhymes chanted on their return, they spent time identifying the trees from their leaves and bark, finding the first flowering daffodils or bluebells, and staying dead while watching a rare red squirrel nibbling on windfallen fruit.

When Úna suggested carving their names high in the oak tree where they sat, Francie had admonished her that you should never leave any trace of having been in a forest or anywhere in nature; humans had already done far too much damage in the world. He loved those woods, and it was in the woods that Úna felt closest to him now that he was far away. The dusty sweetness of the gently decaying forest floor was a balm to her stormy thoughts. Her footsteps slowed, barely disturbing the fallen leaves. She found their oak tree, reached for the lowest branch, swinging her legs against the trunk to find some traction to aid her ascent. She was no longer a girl, amazed now at how easily she had climbed the tree when she was and frustrated with her lack of strength and agility. Nonetheless, before too long, despite aching arms and scratched legs, Úna sat on the branch where she and Francie had often sat, on the branch where he had shakily taken a ring box from his pocket and asked her to marry him. She straddled the sinewy limb and edged her bottom to the trunk; she rested her back against the trunk and pulled her legs up to her chest. The oak had its own scent, and it was Francie's. As she breathed in the scent, their life together played like a silent reel in her head. She had always known him; everyone knew each other in such a small village, but Francie had always been more. There would never be anyone else she would marry; from birth, they were bound together as with some invisible string. A voice, "Úna," made her realise that she had begun to doze on the tree branch, but when she opened her eyes, there was no one there. A single blackbird perched at the end of the branch, head cocked as if examining this rare creature in its tree. "Hello, Mr Blackbird," whispered Úna. The bird hopped off the branch and flew higher into the tree. Úna edged her way down off the branch and made for home, recalling how her father had told her that blackbirds mate for life.

Back on her lane, Mrs Martin was alone, arms crossed leaning on her garden gate. "How are you, Mrs Martin?" said Úna, feeling bad for ignoring her earlier.

"Hello, love," replied Mrs Martin, "I'm sure it was a shock for you."

"What's that?" asked Úna.

"The teacher dying. Didn't he teach your Michael the fiddle for a while?"

Úna's world tilted. "What happened to him?"

"Fell down the stairs, it seems."

Úna tried to run home, but her legs could barely keep her from falling to the ground. She stumbled, tripped, and pulled herself up; she had to cling to the garden posts, fences and gates to drag herself home. When she opened the door, a fiddle played a tune the likes of which she had never heard. It could have been

111

the devil himself playing a tune so fast and full of menace. She slammed the front door, throwing her back against it and sliding to the floor. She screamed into the house, "For God's sake, give me back my son!" But the music only played louder and faster.

Úna got into bed and pulled the blankets over her head. An imposter had changed places with her son. Getting rid of the fiddle, which obviously drew him to this world, had failed. He had thought nothing of disposing of a man to get another fiddle to continue his playing. She had to separate him from the fiddle permanently. She had to do it on Halloween. A plan came to her, an awful plan. A plan which might well damn her soul.

A colder Halloween Úna could not recall. From morning, a deep fog enclosed her lane, its fingers poking in through cracks in the old house. Through the window, the ruddy colours of autumn were hidden. Dark, sodden branches prodded through the mire, clutching ruby leaves. Each house in the lane emitted grey smoke from their brick chimneys, blackened ringlets hanging in the swampy fog. Indoors, Úna had the fire burning since dawn, barely distinct from the night. She hung paper chains in links of purple, orange and green. Her kitchen table was sagging beneath the weight of tarts, loaves, sweets and nuts. In the centre of the room hung a cord ready to be attached to a green apple. On her head, perched the pointed hat she wore every year, and a black cape embroidered with silver moons and stars was tied around her neck. As darkness fell, the older children arrived at her door, chanting and already giddy in their sugar rushes. She called him downstairs. He wore a tunic made from a potato sack, tied at his waist with something long, shiny and sticky; over his face was pulled a thick stocking with three holes roughly torn for his eyes and mouth. He had fastened two rabbit ears on his head, crusty with blood, where he had sewn them to his stocking mask.

"Would you like to come in and play a few games with us, kids?" Úna asked the children at her door. The children looked at him and hesitated as his stockinged face pulled a wide grin. "We have plenty of sweets to fill those baskets," she added. The children came slowly indoors. Úna tied a green apple to the cord hanging from the ceiling. She gave the children slices of apple pie and toffee apples. They played game after game. Úna filled their baskets.

"One last game, you have to play Snap Apple on Halloween!" Each child was blindfolded, one by one, their hands tied behind their backs, and they were spun three times before trying to bite into the coin-encrusted apple. When Michael's turn came around, and he was blindfolded, Úna put her finger to her lips and pointed at the door for the children to leave. She smiled as they looked confused and she mouthed, "It's just a game," and ushered them through the door with one hand, spinning him with the other. When the last child left, she stopped spinning him, and he nodded and nodded, trying to bite into the apple. She ripped the blindfold from his face. She held his fiddle. He tried to reach out, but his hands were tied. She flung the instrument into the blazing fire. He rushed towards the fiddle. Her foot flew out. He fell into the fire, his head thudding on the grate. He leapt up. His head was a fiery Medusa. Melted nylon clumped in flaming lumps on his head. His tunic was ablaze. His angry, fiery form began to fill the whole room.

Úna ran into the kitchen and flung open the back door. Thick, dank fog rolled in through her house; it filled every space. The only thing she could see was him until the miasma quelled the flames, and he shrunk into a smouldering smudge in the murk. A high-pitched whistle pierced her eardrums. A gale thundered into her home. She could see nothing, could hear only the screams of him. All at once, her house was in darkness and silence. As her eyes adjusted, she saw curled in a ball on the floor in the middle of the room, a boy dressed in a red tracksuit. Michael was home.

The next morning, Úna woke up late. Michael was still fast asleep when she checked on him. She sat at the little square window, looking out onto the woods behind her house. The sky was an icy blue, cloudless. The wind shook the last leaves from the trees. Fire blazed in the grate; the room was scented by the sweet, smouldering turf. Úna had not felt this safe since Francie was alive. In her mind, she could see their oak tree and Francie there, swinging his legs off the lowest branch. The dining room door opened slowly, and a sleepy-eyed Michael poked his head around it. She smiled the biggest smile as she went to him and wrapped him in her arms.

"I love you, Michael," she said.

"Me too. Ma?"

"What, son?"

"Where is my fiddle?"

ACKNOWLEDGEMENTS

I would like to thank my loyal gang of first readers, especially Kathryn and Sorley, for their feedback and encouragement, and for ignoring my copious typos. Thanks to my team at UK Book Publishing for their guidance and expertise. Special thanks to Phil for giving me the time and space to scribble, and to Lucy the JRT for snoring at my feet and preventing my escape from many a blank computer screen.

Heartfelt thanks go to my mother for her nightly story reading, probably long after I was too old for bedtime stories, and to my father for his storytelling which is a gift I will always treasure.

Printed in Dunstable, United Kingdom

63915527R10068